THE LAYING ON
of HANDS

D0104943

ALSO BY ALAN BENNETT

FICTION

The Clothes They Stood Up In

PLAYS

Plays One (Forty Years On, Getting On, Habeas Corpus, Enjoy)

Plays Two (Kafka's Dick, the Insurance Man, The Old Country, An Englishman Abroad, A Question of Attribution)

Office Suite
The Wind in the Willows
The Madness of King George III
The Lady in the Van

TELEVISION PLAYS

The Writer in Dialogue
Objects of Affection (BBC)
Talking Heads (BBC)

SCREENPLAYS

A Private Function
Prick Up Your Ears
The Madness of King George

AUTOBIOGRAPHIES

The Lady in the Van
Writing Home

THE LAYING ON
of HANDS

Stories

ALAN BENNETT

Picador
New York

www.picadorusa.com

Picador® is a U.S. registered trademark and is used by St. Martin's Press
under license from Pan Books Limited.

For information on Picador Reading Group Guides, as well as ordering, please
contact the Trade Marketing department at St. Martin's Press.
Phone: 1-800-221-7945 extension 763
Fax: 212-677-7456
E-mail: trademarketing@stmartins.com

"The Laying On of Hands" was first published in Great Britain
by Profile Books, under the title *The Laying On of Hands.*

"Miss Fozzard Finds Her Feet" was first published in Great Britain
by BBC as part of *Talking Heads 2.*

"Father! Father! Burning Bright" was first published in Great Britain
by Profile Books, under the title *Father! Father! Burning Bright.*

Library of Congress Cataloging-in-Publication Data

Bennett, Alan.
        The laying on of hands : stories / Alan Bennett
            p. cm.
        Contents: The laying on of hands—Miss Fozzard finds her feet—Father!
Father! Burning bright.
        ISBN 0-312-29051-9 (hc)
        ISBN 0-312-42225-3 (pbk)
        1. Great Britain—Social life and customs—20th century—Fiction.
I. Title.

PR6052.E5 L39 2002
823'.914—dc21   2001059050

First Picador Paperback Edition: May 2003

10 9 8 7 6 5 4 3 2 1

Contents

The Laying On

of Hands

Seated obscurely towards the back of the church and on a side aisle, Treacher was conscious nevertheless of being much looked at. Tall, thin and with a disagreeable expression, were this a film written forty years ago he would have been played by the actor Raymond Huntley who, not unvinegary in life, in art made a speciality of ill-tempered businessmen and officious civil servants. Treacher was neither but he, too, was nothing to look at. Yet several times he caught women (and it was women particularly) bending forward in their seats to get a better view of him across the aisle; a murmured remark passed between a couple in front, the woman then turning round, ostensibly to take in the architecture but actually to look at him, whereas others in the congregation dispensed with such polite circumspection and just stared.

Unwelcome enough in any circumstances, this scrutiny was not at all what Treacher had had in mind when he had come into the church fully half an hour before the service was due to start, a precaution against having his hand shaken at the door by the vicar. Such redundant clerical conviviality was always distasteful to Treacher but on this occasion he had a particular reason for avoiding it. Luckily the vicar was not to be seen but, early as he was, Treacher had still had to run the gauntlet of a woman in the porch, a reporter presumably, who was making a record of those attending the memorial service. She held out her book for him to sign.

'Name and organisation?'

But Treacher had pushed past as if she were a lowlier form of autograph hunter. 'Not important,' he said, though whether he meant he was not important or that it was not important his name be recorded was not plain.

'I'll put you under "and many other friends",' she had called after him, though in fact he had never met the deceased and did not even know his name.

Somewhere out of the way was what he wanted, where he could see and not be seen and well back on the side aisle he thought he had found it, instead of which the fuller the church became the more he seemed the focus of attention. It was very vexing.

In fact no one was looking at Treacher at all, except when they pretended to look at him in order also to take in someone sitting in the row behind. A worldlier man than Treacher, if worldliness consists in watching television, would have known why. Seated behind him was a thick-set shaven-headed young man in dark glasses, black suit and black T-shirt who, minus the shades and occasionally (and far too rarely some viewers felt) minus the T-shirt, appeared nightly on the nation's screens in a television soap. The previous week he had stunned his audience when, with no excuse whatsoever, he had raped his mother, and though it later transpired she had been begging for it for some time and was actually no relation at all, nevertheless some vestiges of the nation's fascinated revulsion still clung to him. In life, though, as he was at pains to point out to any chat-show host who would listen, he was a pussy-cat and indeed, within minutes of the maternal rape, he could be found on another channel picking out the three items of antique furniture he would invest in were his budget limited to £500.

None of this Treacher knew, only becoming aware

of the young man when an usher spotted him and insisted on shepherding the modest hunk to a more prominent seat off the centre aisle next to a chef who, though famously disgruntled in the workplace, now smilingly shifts along to accommodate the big-thighed newcomer. After his departure Treacher was relieved, though not unpuzzled, to find himself invisible once more and so able to look unobserved at the incoming congregation.

There was quite a throng, with people still crowding through the door and a small queue now stretching over the worn and greasy gravestones that paved this London churchyard. The flanks of the queue were harried by autograph hunters and the occasional photographer, outlying celebrities meekly signing as they shuffled on towards the door. One or two did refuse, on the justifiable grounds that this wasn't a first night (and more of a closing than an opening), but the autograph hunters were impatient of such scruples, considering themselves wilfully thwarted. 'Choosy cow,' one muttered as he turned away from some glacial TV newsreader, brightening only when he spotted an ageing disc jockey he had thought long since dead.

The huddled column pressed on up the steps.

As memorial services go these days it had been billed

as 'a celebration', the marrying of the valedictory with the festive convenient on several grounds. For a start it made grief less obligatory, which was useful as the person to be celebrated had been dead some time and tears would have been something of an acting job. To call it a celebration also allowed the congregation to dress up not down, so that though the millinery might be more muted, one could have been forgiven, thought Treacher, for thinking this was a wedding not a wake.

Clive Dunlop, the dead man, was quite young—34 according to the dates given on the front of the Order of Service, though there were some in the congregation who had thought him even younger. Still, it was a shocking age to die, there was no disagreement about that and what little conviviality there might have been was muffled accordingly.

Knowing the deceased, many of those filing into the church in surprisingly large numbers also knew each other, though in the circumstances prevailing at funerals and memorial services this is not always easy to tell as recognition tends to be kept to a minimum—the eye downcast, the smile on hold, any display of pleasure at the encounter or even shared grief postponed until the business of the service is done—however sad the professionally buoyant clergyman will generally assure the congregation that that business is not going to be.

True, there were a number of extravagant one-word embraces, 'Bless!' for instance, and even 'Why?', a despairing invocation that seemed more appropriate for the actual interment which (though nobody seemed quite to know where) appeared to have taken place some six months previously. Extravagant expressions of sorrow seemed out of place here, if only because a memorial service, as the clergyman will generally insist, is a positive occasion, the negative side of the business (though they seldom come out baldly with this) over and done with at the disposal of the body. Because, however upbeat a priest manages to be (and indeed his creed requires him to be), it's hard not to feel that cheerful though the memorial service can be, the actual interment does tend to be a bit of a downer.

Still, discreet funerals and extravagant memorial services are not unusual these days, the finality of death mitigated by staggering it over two stages. 'Of course there'll be a memorial service,' people say, excusing their non-attendance at the emotionally more demanding (and socially less enjoyable) obsequies. And it is generally the case nowadays that anybody who is anybody is accorded a memorial service—and some-times an anybody who isn't.

Hard to say what Clive was, for instance, though tak-ing note of the numerous celebrities who were still filing in, 'well-connected' would undoubtedly describe him.

Dubbing such a service a celebration was, thought Treacher, a mistake as it could be thought to license a degree of whoopee. The Order of Service included a saxophone solo, which was ominous, and Treacher's misgivings were confirmed when a young man sat down heavily in the pew in front, laid his Order of Service on the ledge then put his cigarettes and lighter beside it.

She was in the next pew, but spotting the cigarettes the spirits of a recently ennobled novelist rose. 'You can smoke,' she whispered.

Her companion shook her head. 'I don't think so.'

'I see no signs saying not. Is that one?'

Fumbling for her spectacles she peered at a plaque affixed to a pillar.

'I think,' said her friend, 'that's one of the Stations of the Cross.'

'Really? Well I'm sure I saw an ashtray as I was coming in.'

'That was holy water.'

In the light of these accessories, more often to be met with in Roman Catholic establishments, it was hardly surprising if some of the congregation were in doubt as to the church's denomination, which was actually Anglican, though a bit on the high side.

'I can smell incense,' said a feared TV interviewer to his actress friend. 'Are we in a Catholic church?'

She had once stabbed a priest to death in a film involving John Mills so knew about churches. 'Yes,' she said firmly.

At which point a plumpish man in a cassock crossed the chancel in order to collect a book from a pew, bowing to the altar en route.

'See that,' said the interviewer. 'The bowing? That's part of the drill. Though it looks a bit pick 'n' mix to me. Mind you, that's the trend these days. Ecumenicalism. I talked to the Pope about it once. Sweet man.'

'I missed the funeral,' whispered one woman to her vaguely known neighbour. 'I didn't even know it had happened.'

'Same with me,' the neighbour whispered back. 'I think it was private. What did he die of?'

The sight of a prominent actor in the Royal Shakespeare Company gliding humbly to an empty place in the front row curtailed further discussion, though it was the prototype of several similar conversations going on in various parts of the church. Other people were trying to recall why it was they had failed to attend a funeral which ought to have been high on their lists. Was it in the provinces they wondered, which would account for it, or one of the obscurer parts of South London . . . Sydenham, say, or Catford, venues that would be a real test of anybody's friendship?

It had actually been in Peru, a fact known to very *few* people in the congregation though in the subdued hum of conversation that preceded the start of the service this news and the unease it generated began to spread. Perhaps out of tact the question, 'What did he die of?' was not much asked and when it was sometimes prompted a quizzical look suggesting it was a question best left unput; that, or a sad smile implying Clive had succumbed not to any particular ailment but to the general tragedy that is life itself.

Spoken or unspoken, the uncertain circumstances of the death, its remote location and the shocking prematureness of it contributed to an atmosphere of gloom and, indeed, apprehension in the church. There was conversation but it was desultory and subdued;

many people's thoughts seemed to be on themselves. Few of them attended a place of worship with any regularity, their only contact with churches occasions like this, which, as was ruefully remarked in several places in the congregation, 'seemed to be happening all too often these days'.

To Treacher, glancing at the details on the front of the Order of Service it was all fairly plain. He was a single man who had died young. Thirty-four. These days there was not much mystery about that.

'He told me 30, the scamp,' said one of the many smart women who was craning round to see who was still coming in. 'But then he would.'

'I thought he was younger,' said someone else. 'But he looked after himself.'

'Not well enough,' said her husband, whose wife's grief had surprised him. 'I never understood where the money came from.'

Anyone looking at the congregation and its celebrity assortment could be forgiven for thinking that Clive had been a social creature. This wasn't altogether true and this numinous gathering studded with household names was less a manifestation of his friendships than an advertisement for his discretion.

It was true that many of those present knew each

other and virtually all of them knew Clive. But that the others knew Clive not all of them knew and only woke up to the fact when they had settled in their seats and started looking round. So while most memorial services take place in an atmosphere of suppressed recognition and reunion to this one was added an element of surprise, many of those present having come along on the assumption they would be among a select few.

Finding this was far from the case the surprise was not untinged with irritation. Or as a go-for-the-throat Australian wordsmith put it to her companion, 'Why, the two-faced pisshole.'

Diffidence was much to the fore. A leading international architect, one of whose airports had recently sprung a leak, came down the centre aisle, waiting at the end of a pew until someone made room, his self-effacing behaviour and downcast eyes proclaiming him a person of some consequence humbled by the circumstances in which he currently found himself and which might have been allegorically represented on a ceiling, say (although not one of his), as Fame deferring to Mortality. 'Do not recognise me,' his look said. 'I am here only to grieve.'

Actually, compared with the soap-stars he hardly

counted as famous at all. The world of celebrity in England, at any rate, is small. Whereas fame in America vaults over the barriers of class and profession, lawyers rubbing shoulders with musicians, politicians and stars of the stage and screen, in England, television apart, celebrity comes in compartments, *Who's Who* not always the best guide to who's who. Thus here Fame did not always recognise Reputation or Beauty Merit.

A high official in the Treasury, for instance, had got himself seated next to a woman who kept consulting her powder compact, her renown as bubbling game-show host as wasted on him as his skill in succinct summation was lost on her. Worlds collided but with no impact at all, so while what few lawyers there were knew the politicians and some of the civil servants, none of them knew the genial wag who pounced on reluctant volunteers and teased out their less than shamefaced confessions on late-night TV. The small-screen gardeners knew the big-screen heart-throbs but none of them recognised 'someone high up in the Bank of England' ('and I don't mean the window-cleaner,' whispered a man who did).

Much noticed, though, was a pop singer who had been known to wear a frock but was today dressed in a suit of stunning sobriety, relieved only by a diamond clasp that had once belonged to Catherine the Great and which was accompanied by an obligatory security guard insisted on by the insurance company. This bovine young man lounged in the pew picking his fingers, happy already to have pinpointed Suspect No. I, the Waynflete Professor of Moral Philosophy in the University of Oxford who, timid though he was, clearly had villain written all over him.

In front of the Professor was a member of the Government, who was startled to find himself opposite his Permanent Secretary, seated on the other side of the aisle.

'I didn't know you knew Dunlop,' the minister said the next day as they plodded through some meeting on carbon monoxide emissions.

'Oh, I knew him from way back,' said the civil servant airily.

'Me too,' said the minister. 'Way back.'

Actually the minister had only met Clive quite recently, just after he became a minister in fact, but this 'way back' in which both of them took refuge was a time so remote and unspecific that anything that might have happened then was implicitly excused by their youth and the temper of the times. 'I knew him in the Sixties' would have been the same, except that Clive was too young for that.

'At some point,' murmured the minister, 'I want you to take me on one side and explain to me the difference between carbon monoxide and carbon dioxide. Fairly star-studded, wasn't it?'

It was, indeed, a remarkable assembly with philanthropy, scholarship and genuine distinction represented alongside much that was tawdry and merely fashionable, so that with only a little licence this stellar, but tarnished throng might, for all its shortcomings, be taken as a version of England.

And 'a very English occasion' was how it was described by the reporter in the *Telegraph* the next day. Not that she was in a position to know as she hadn't bothered to stay for the service. Currently taking down the names of the last few stragglers she compiled her list, procured a programme of the proceedings, then went off to the Design Museum to lunch with a colleague.

'After all,' she said over oeufs en gêlée, 'they're all the same these occasions. Like sad cocktail parties without the drinks.'

This one as it turned out wasn't, so she got the sack. But it was a nice lunch.

Also thinking how English these occasions tended to be was the young priest in charge, Father Geoffrey Jolliffe. Father Jolliffe was Anglican but with Romish inclinations that were not so much doctrinal as ceremonial and certainly sartorial. Amiable, gregarious and plump, he looked well in the cloak he generally went about in, a priest with a bit of a swish to him. His first curacy had been in a slum parish where, as he put it, 'They like a bit of that,' and since he did too, his ministry got off to a good start and that he chose to call the Eucharist 'Mass' and himself 'Father' troubled no one. His present parish, St Andrew Upchance on the borders of Shoreditch and the City, was also poor, but he had done a good deal to 'turn it round', an achievement that had not gone unnoticed in the diocese, where he was spoken of as a coming man.

There were, it is true, some of his fellow clergy who found him altogether too much, but as he said himself, 'There's not enough of "too much" these days,' and since he was a lively preacher and old-fashioned when it came to the prayer book, a large and loyal congregation seemed to bear this out.

Used at his normal services to women predominating, today Father Jolliffe was not altogether surprised to find so many men turning up. Some of them had been close to Clive, obviously, but that apart, in his experience men needed less cajoling to attend funerals and memorial services than they did normal church (or even the theatre, say) and since men seldom do what they don't want, it had made him wonder why. He decided that where the dead were involved there was always an element of condescension: the deceased had been put in his or her place, namely the grave, and however lavish the tributes with which this was accompanied there was no altering the fact that the situation of the living was altogether superior and to men, in particular, that seemed to appeal.

USUALLY CHEERFUL and expansive, today Father Jolliffe was preoccupied. He had known Clive himself, which accounted for his church being the somewhat out of the way venue for the memorial service. His death had come as an unpleasant surprise, as, like so many in the congregation, he had not known Clive was even ill. It was sad, too, of course, 'a shared sadness' as he planned to say, but for him, as for others in the congregation, it was somewhat worrying also (though he had no plans to say that).

Still, if he was anxious he did not intend to let it affect his performance. 'And,' as he had recently insisted to a Diocesan Selection Board, 'a service is a performance. Devout, sincere and given wholeheartedly for God, but a performance nevertheless.'

The Board, on the whole, had been impressed.

By coincidence the subject of memorial services had come up at the Board when Father Jolliffe, suppressing a fastidious shudder, had heard himself describe such occasions as 'a challenge'. Urged to expand he had shared his vision of the church packed with unaccustomed worshippers come together, as they thought, simply to commemorate a loved one but also (though they might not know it) hungering for that hope and reassurance which it was the clergy's job to satisfy. This, too, had gone down well with the Board though most of them, Father Jolliffe included, knew it was tosh.

The truth was memorial services were a bugger. For all its shortcomings in the way of numbers a regular congregation was in church because it wanted to be or at least felt it ought to be. It's true that looking down from the pulpit on his flock Sunday by Sunday

Father Jolliffe sometimes felt that God was not much more than a pastime; that these were churchgoers as some people were pigeon-fanciers or collectors of stamps, gentle, mildly eccentric and hanging onto the end of something. Still, on a scale ranging from fervent piety to mere respectability these regular worshippers were at least like-minded: they had come together to worship God and even with their varying degrees of certainty that there was a God to worship the awkward question of belief seldom arose.

With a memorial service, and a smart one at that, God was an embarrassment and Father Jolliffe was reminded of this when he had his first sight of the congregation. He had left his service book in his stall and nipping across to get it before putting on his robes he was taken aback at the packed and murmuring pews. Few of those attending, he suspected, had on taking their seats bowed their heads in prayer or knew that that was (once anyway) the form. Few would know the hymns, and still fewer the prayers. Yet he was shortly going to have to stand up and ask them to collaborate in the fiction that they all believed in God (or something anyway) and even that there was an after-life. So what he had said to the Board had been right. It was a challenge, the challenge being that most of them would think this an insult to their intelligence.

How Father Jolliffe was going to cope with this dilemma was interesting Treacher. Indeed it was partly what had brought him to St Andrew's on this particular morning. There were various ways round it, the best of which, in Treacher's view, was not to get round it at all; ignore it in fact, a priest retaining more respect if he led the congregation in prayer with neither explanation nor apology, the assumption being that they were all believers and if not, since they were in the house of God, it behoved them to pretend to be so. Taking the uncompromising line, though, meant that it was hard then for the clergyman to get on those friendly, informal terms with the congregation that such an occasion seemed to require. Treacher did not see this as a drawback. A priest himself, although in mufti, getting on friendly terms with the congregation had never been high on his list.

Father Jolliffe would not have agreed. 'Whatever else it is,' he had told the Board, 'a congregation is first and foremost an audience. And I am the stand-up. I must win them over.' It was another bold-seeming sentiment that had hit the spot, occasioning some laughter, it's true, but also much sage nodding, though not, Father Jolliffe had noticed, from Canon Treacher, who was an archdeacon and not enthusiastic about congregations in the first place. Treacher (and his fiercely sharpened pencil) was the only one of the Board who had made him nervous (the Bishop was a sweetie), so it was a blessing that on this particular morning, thanks to Canon Treacher's precautions, the priest remained unaware of his presence.

The worst tack a priest could adopt at a service such as this, and a trap Treacher was pretty confident Father Jolliffe was going to fall into, was to acknowledge at the start that the congregation (or 'friends' as Treacher had even heard them called) might not subscribe to the beliefs implicit in the hymns and prayers but that they should on no account feel badly about this but instead substitute appropriate sentiments of their own. ('I believe this stuff but you don't have to.') Since in Treacher's experience there would be few in the church with appropriate sentiments still less beliefs to hand, this meant that if the congregation thought of anything at all during the prayers (which he doubted) it was just to try and summon up a picture of the departed sufficient to squeeze out the occasional tear.

Treacher, it has to be said, had some reason for his

pessimism. Casting an eye over the Order of Service Treacher noted that in addition to a saxophone solo a fashionable baritone from Covent Garden was down to sing 'Some Enchanted Evening'. With such delights in prospect Father Treacher feared that liturgical rigour would not be high on the list.

What approach he was going to take to the service ('what angle the priest should come at it') Father Jolliffe had not yet decided, though since he was even now being robed in the vestry it might be thought there was not much time. But he had never been methodical, his sermon often no more than a few headings or injunctions to himself on the back of the parish notes: though on this occasion he had not even bothered with that, preferring, as he would have said, to 'wing it'. This was less slipshod than it sounded, as he genuinely believed that in this 'winging' there was an element of the divine. He had never thought it out but felt that the wings were God-sent, an angel's possibly, or another version of 'Thy wings' under the shadow of which he bade the faithful hide Sunday by Sunday.

He slipped out of the vestry and made his way round the outside of the church to join the choir now assembled at the West door. When he had been appointed vicar at St Andrew's processions generally began obscurely at the vestry winding their awkward way round past the pulpit and up the chancel steps. Father Jolliffe felt that this was untheatrical and missing a trick so one of his first innovations was to make the entrance of the choir and clergy bolder and more dramatic, routeing the procession down the centre of the church.

The procession should have been headed and the choir preceded by a crucifer bearing the processional cross (another innovation), but since this was a weekday Leo, the crucifer, had not been able to get time off work. A beefy young man, Leo was a bus driver and Father Jolliffe had always taken quiet pride in that fact and would occasionally cite him at diocesan conferences as a modern update of the calling of the disciples ('Matthew may have been a tax-collector. What's so special about that? Our crucifer happens to be a bus driver'). Though Leo would much have preferred marching down the centre aisle to where he currently was, stuck behind the wheel of a No. 74 inching up Putney High Street, since privatisation religious obligation was no longer accepted as a reason for absence. 'Or believe me, my son,' said the supervisor, 'come Ramadan and our Sikh and Hindu brethren who compose a substantial proportion of the workforce would be up at the mosque when we need them down at the depot. I'm not without religious feeling myself and my sister-in-law was nearly a nun but sorry, no can do.'

Still, what the procession lacked in splendour at the front it made up in dignity at the back, as in addition to Father Jolliffe also attending the service were several other clergymen, one of them indeed a suffragan bishop. None of them was personally known to Father Jolliffe or seemingly to each other, but all were presumably known to Clive. Though got up in all their gear they were not attending in any official capacity (and in the *Telegraph* report of the occasion they would be described as 'robed and in the sanctuary'), but they definitely brought a kick to the rear of the column which was now assembled and waiting to begin its journey towards the chancel.

The organist was meanwhile playing an arrangement of Samuel Barber's Adagio for Strings which many in the congregation were enjoying, having been made familiar with the tune from its frequent airings on Classic FM. Seeing no conclusion in the offing Father Jolliffe pressed a button behind a pillar to alert the organist that they were ready to begin. The Barber now came to a sharp and unceremonious close but since random terminations were not unusual on Classic FM, nobody noticed.

Now from somewhere at the back of the church Father Jolliffe's voice rang out, 'Would you stand?' and the church shuffled to its feet. 'We shall sing the first hymn on your Order of Service, "Love Divine All Loves Excelling".'

Once upon a time it would have been enough to announce the hymn and the congregation would have known to stand. Hymns you stand, prayers you kneel. Nowadays it was prayers you sit, hymns you wait and see what other people are going to do. 'Love,' Father Jolliffe reproached himself. 'We must love one another.'

Now the clergy began to follow the choir down the aisle, Father Jolliffe bringing up the rear, singing the hymn without consulting the words, long since off the book and thus free while singing heartily to cast professionally loving glances to right and left, on his pink and generous face an expression of settled benevolence.

He had still not decided how to pitch his opening remarks, trusting even now that something would occur, in some ways the closest he got to faith in God this trust that when it came to the point words would be put into his mouth. As he passed through the worshippers raggedly singing the hymn, Father Jolliffe thought they looked less like a congregation than an audience, smart, worldly and doubtless expecting him to keep God very much on the back burner. He resented this a little, because, though he was a sophisticated priest and too self-forgiving, his faith was real enough, though so supple and riddled with irony that God was no more exempt from censure than the Archbishop of Canterbury (whom he privately referred to as Old Potato-Face). Still, he resented having to tailor his beliefs to his audience and not for the first time wished he was an out and out Catholic where this problem wouldn't arise. One of the many grumbles Father Jolliffe had about the English Reformation was that it was then that feeling had got into the service, so you couldn't get away with just saying the words but had to mean them at the same time.

These thoughts had taken him and the procession to the chancel, where the choir filed into their pews and the spare clergy disposed themselves around, while still leaving the hymn with a couple of verses to run. This gave Father Jolliffe a chance to think about what he ought to say about Clive and what he ought not to say.

. . .

CLIVE HAD BEEN A MASSEUR; there was no secret
about that. It was something he was very good at and
his skill transcended mere physical manipulation. Many
of his clients attested to a feeling of warmth that
seemed to flow through his fingers and for which there
was no orthodox physiological explanation. 'He has
healing hands' was one way of putting it or (this from
the more mystically inclined) 'He has the Touch.'

That Clive was black (though palely so) was thought
by some to account for these healing attributes since it
meant (despite his having been born and brought up
in Bethnal Green) that he was closer to his origins than
were his clients and in touch with an ancient wisdom
long since lost to them. Never discouraging these
mythic speculations Clive himself had no such illu-
sions, though the pouch to which he stripped to carry
out the massage was rudimentary enough to call up all
sorts of primitive musings.

The heat that his clients felt, though, was not fan-
ciful and as a boy had embarrassed Clive and made
him reluctant to touch or be touched. The realisation
that what he had was not a burden but a gift was a

turning point and that, with his calorific propensities, it could be marketed was another. And so the laying on of hands became for him a way of life.

There was, of course, more. Though Clive was scrupulous never to omit the ceremony of massage, for some it was just the preliminary to a more protracted and intimate encounter and one which might, understandably, cost them a little more. Looking over the crowded church, Father Jolliffe wondered who were here just as grateful patients whose burden of pain Clive had smoothed away and who had come along to commemorate the easing of a different sort of burden, and of the latter how many were as nervous as he was himself about the legacy that the dead man might have left them.

NOW AS THE HYMN ENDED Father Jolliffe said, 'Will you sit?', gave them a moment to settle and then launched into his preamble. And straightaway came out with something he had no intention of saying.

'On such occasions as these,' he said, 'a priest will often preface his remarks with an apology, craving the forgiveness of the congregation since they have had the advantage of knowing the deceased whereas he didn't.

I make no such apology. I knew Clive and like most of you, I imagine, loved him and valued his friendship—else why are any of us here?'

Treacher, who was not here for that at all, made a neat note on the back of his Order of Service.

Father Jolliffe was amazed at himself. Few people in the congregation were aware he knew Clive and for various reasons, one of which was prudence, he hadn't been planning to say that he did. Now he had blurted it out and must make the best of it, though this would be hard as there was so much he could not say.

For the most part Geoffrey (and there are some circumstances in which it's right he is called Geoffrey and not Father Jolliffe) . . . for the most part Geoffrey was celibate, though he attached no virtue to this, knowing it was not abstinence so much as lack of opportunity that kept him generally unconjugate; that and a certain timidity where sex was concerned which made him, despite his (mild) moral disapproval, bestow on an enterprising promiscuity such as Clive's an almost heroic status. No matter that boldness came as naturally to Clive as diffidence did to Geoffrey or that Clive, of course, was much better looking and unburdened by Geoffrey's thoughts of God (and not looking a fool); Geoffrey knew that in what nowadays is called a one-to-one situation he was what he thought of as shy, so that men who weren't shy, such as Clive, seemed to him warriors, their valour, however profligate, more of a virtue than his own timorous drawing back.

Geoffrey had had experience at first hand of how fly Clive could be. En route for lunch together along the Farringdon Road (not a thoroughfare Geoffrey had ever thought of in a carnal context) Clive had intercepted a male glance that Geoffrey had not even noticed and quick as a fish he had darted away leaving Geoffrey to eat alone and return home disconsolate, where Clive duly came by to give an account of his afternoon. True, Clive was not choosy or how else would he have got into bed with Geoffrey himself, episodes so decorous that for Clive they can scarcely have registered as sex at all, though still tactile enough for Geoffrey, on the news of Clive's death, to be filled with unease.

Being of an Anglo-Catholic persuasion Father Jolliffe practised auricular confession, when he would come clean about his predilections, an ordeal that was somewhat diminished by choosing as his confessor a clergyman whom he knew 'had no problem with that' and being of a similar persuasion himself would place it low down in the hierarchy of possible wickedness.

With never much to confess on that particular score, now with Clive gone there was going to be even less.

Somebody coughed. The congregation were waiting and though the pause while Father Jolliffe wrestled with what he should and should not say was understood to be one of deep personal remembrance or even a chance to regain control of his feelings, still, there wasn't all day.

Father Jolliffe plunged on and suddenly it all came right. 'We shall be singing some hymns. We shall pray together and there will be readings and some of Clive's favourite music.' Father Jolliffe paused. 'Prayer may seem to some of you an outmoded activity and hymns too, possibly, but that was not what Clive thought. Clive, as I know personally, was always keen to involve himself in the rites and rituals of the church and were he here he would be singing louder and praying harder than anybody.'

Despite the unintentional disclosure of his friendship with Clive, Father Jolliffe was not displeased with how he (or possibly God) had turned it to good account. Using Clive as a way round any misgivings the congregation might have re the religious side of things was a happy thought. It took the curse off the service very nicely and in the shadows behind the pillar Treacher made another note and this time added a tick.

Actually Geoffrey (we are back to Geoffrey again) knew that where Clive's religious inclinations were concerned he was stretching it a bit. Pious he wasn't and his interest in the rites and rituals of the church didn't go much further than the not unfetching young men who were often helping to perform them, Clive reckoning, not always correctly, that what with the ceremony, the incense and the general dressing-up any-one of a religious disposition was, as he put it, 'halfway there already'. He was particularly keen on vestments, though not in any way Father Jolliffe (sorry) could share with the congregation, having once found Clive in the rectory clad only in his underpants trying on cotta and cope.

Father Jolliffe now led the congregation in prayer, asking them to kneel if they so chose or simply bow their heads so that they could together remember Clive. Heads went down, eyes were closed with only the security guard on the qui vive, scowling across the bowed benches where someone, he felt sure, might be only pretending to pray. At one point he even stood up and turned round lest some wrongdoer might be

taking advantage of these unstructured devotions in order to creep up and snatch the clasp. Suspicious, as he
put it, 'of this whole prayer thing' he slumped back
moodily in his seat as Jolliffe launched into the Collect.

The vicar didn't improvise prayers, Treacher was relieved to note, drawing them from the ample stock of
the old prayer book, and saying them briskly and formally as Treacher preferred them to be said. There
were few things worse, in Treacher's view, than a priest
who gave too much weight to the words of prayers,
pausing as if to invest them with heartfelt meaning and
thereby impressing the congregation (and himself) with
his sincerity. Treacher had even heard the Lord's Prayer
delivered in this fashion and found it intolerable and
even queasy. But Father Jolliffe, perhaps because of his
Catholic leanings, was dry and to the point. 'Say the
word, say the word only' seemed to be his motto and
Treacher added another tick.

So far, Treacher was bound to admit, Jolliffe was
not doing too badly. Even the news of the priest's
friendship with the dead man had scarcely counted
against him, as the Archdeacon had all along assumed
Jolliffe to be homosexual, though without seeing this
as a cause for censure or even a necessary obstacle to

promotion. Untrammelled by wife or family and with a housekeeper to look after the vicarage (when there were vicarages to look after), their energies channelled, the sex under wraps, once upon a time homosexuals had made excellent priests and still could so long as they were sensible. The homosexuals Treacher preferred were dry, acerbic and, of course, unavowed; A. E. Housman the type that he approved of, minus the poetry, of course, and (though this was less important) minus the atheism. Nowadays, though, discretion had been cast aside and it had all gone splashy, priests feeling in conscience bound to make their proclivities plain, with even Jolliffe's declaration of friendship for the dead man a timorous attempt, Treacher felt, to lay his cards on the table. Which was a mistake, Treacher believing that a priest should no more declare a sexual preference than he should a political one. Even so, Treacher reflected, there was this to be said in Jolliffe's favour that, whatever his shortcomings, he was not she. In Treacher's church there was a place for she, running the jumble sale, or doing the altar flowers; a she could even take the plate round or read the lesson. But there was no place for she at the altar or in the pulpit. So, give Jolliffe his due: he was not she.

. . .

Now the congregation sat and the scheduled part of the service began. The programme had been put together by Pam, a cheerful woman Clive had known since childhood and who was now a producer at the BBC, and Derek, his longtime landlord. Eclectic would be the kindest word to describe it. Treacher, who had no reason to be kind, thought it looked a bit of a ragbag.

First up was a well-known actress and star of a current sitcom who ascends the stairs of the lectern where she reads immaculately a piece about death not really being the end but just like popping next door. It was a regular standard at memorial services and seeing it billed in the programme Treacher had sighed. He believed in death and when he said he believed in God, death was to a large extent what he meant. These days people didn't, or tried not to, always feeling death was unfair, so when they saw it coming to them or their loved ones they made a great song and dance about it.

And these days there was always blame; it was 'down to' someone or other—the school, the doctor, the police—and you must fight back, that was today's philosophy; in the midst of life we are in death was nowadays a counsel for wimps. It didn't used to be like this, he thought. Had it come from America, he wondered. Or Liverpool? Was television to blame? Or Mrs Thatcher? These days he seldom felt well himself but he wasn't complaining. Or perhaps (and here he was trying to be charitable) what was really distasteful was death as leveller. These days people were so anxious to lay hold of anything that marked them out from the rest—the death of their children, for instance, their neglect by hospitals, being fumbled when young or tortured by nuns; even the murder of loved ones would do if it served to single them out. Whereas the good thing about death was that it singled everybody out. It was the one unchanging thing. Treacher smiled.

Father Jolliffe's thoughts were different, though just as wayward and far from Clive. The next reader had a ponytail and Geoffrey found himself wondering at what point in bed the hair was unloosed, shaken out, let down. And by whom? He thought of the curtain of hair falling across the pillow, the signal, perhaps (in addition to other signals), that the body was now on offer. So again he remembered Clive.

Next up was a pianist, another personal acquaintance who comes to the piano in mittens which he then takes off before playing some Schubert, the performance of which, judging by his expression, seems to cause him exquisite pain but which turns to dark-faced anger as during the final section a police car drives past with its siren going.

And so it goes on, under Father Jolliffe's benevolent eye, poems, readings, a succession of 'turns' really, one of which, though, Treacher is pleased to note, is from St Paul's First Letter to the Corinthians, the passage about love, with Father Jolliffe opting for the King James version using charity. He took time at the start of the reading to explain to the congregation that charity was love and not anything to do with flag days or people in doorways. Or if it was to do with people in doorways that was only one of its meanings.

Treacher would have scorned such condescension and let the congregation make of it what they could but he forbore to mark his card on the point. Still, he would have preferred it if the great rolling cadences of the Authorised Version hadn't been followed by a saxophone rendition of the Dusty Springfield standard, 'You don't have to say you love me', a number (and there was no other word for it) that occasioned a round of applause, from which Treacher unsurprisingly abstained.

During the saxophone solo Geoffrey's worries about Clive recurred. What had he died of? He wished he knew for certain. Or not. Geoffrey had been in bed with Clive seldom and so tamely that only someone as inexperienced as Geoffrey would have thought himself at risk at all. But it did happen, he knew that; he wasn't even sure if there was some risk in kissing (though there hadn't been much of that either).

The truth was it was God that Geoffrey didn't trust. Irony was always the deity's strong point and to afflict a transgressor as timid as Geoffrey with such a disproportionate penalty might appeal to the Almighty's sense of cosmic fun. It was unfair to God, he knew, but he'd always felt the deity had a mean side and on one of his reports at theological college his tutor had written, 'Tends to confuse God with Joan Crawford.'

Treacher looked at his watch. One or two of the participants had preceded their contributions with a few words about Clive—Clive as assiduous and imaginative hospital visitor, Clive as holiday companion, Clive as lover of Schubert and dogs. Still, though these had lengthened the proceedings a little, Treacher was relieved to note that they were now on the last item before the final hymn, a rendering by an ancient musical comedy actress of 'darling Ivor's' immortal 'Fly home, little heart'. 'Fly home, Clive,' she prefaced it, 'our thoughts go with you.'

As her quavering soprano drifted through the church, Treacher began to make plans to slip away as unobtrusively as he had arrived. Slightly to the Archdeacon's regret he had to concede that Father Jolliffe had not done too badly. He had kept the service moving and each contribution brief: he had not sold God short and even allowing for the saxophone solo and the old lady currently in full, if tiny, voice it had never ceased to be a church service. Treacher had come along hoping to find Father Jolliffe a bit of a clown and over-anxious to please. There had been no evidence of that and he deserved credit. Canon Treacher folded his Order of Service and put it in his pocket. He would nip out during the last hymn.

FATHER JOLLIFFE, too, was pleased the service was over in such good time, though he had some regrets. Varied though the contributions had been he didn't feel they had done justice to Clive and his special charm. Nobody had quite captured his character; an opportunity had been missed. Besides, Father Jolliffe (and he can surely be forgiven) was still somewhat star-

struck by his glamorous congregation and understandably wanted to hold onto them for just a little longer.
They were such a change from his usual attendance
who (while just as precious in the sight of God, of
course) were drabber and less fun.

So when the old lady finished and was greeted with
such sympathetic applause she had to be coaxed from
the microphone before she got into an encore, Father
Jolliffe on a sudden impulse (with which he subsequently thought God had had something to do) didn't
sink to his knees for the final prayers but stood up,
moved to the centre of the chancel steps and expressed
the hope that anyone with cherished memories of
Clive which they would like to share should now feel
free to do so. Treacher frowned and fished the Order
of Service out of his pocket to check that this was a
departure from the published proceedings. Finding that
it was and the proceedings had indeed been prolonged
he put a large question-mark in the margin.

Father Jolliffe stood on the chancel steps and in the
expectant silence the ponderous workings of the clock,
fixed on the back wall of the tower, now began to click
and whirr preparatory to slowly striking 12. From experience Father Jolliffe knew that these crankings made
speech impossible, so hearing those first admonitory

clicks he had learned to pause and wait until the ancient mechanism had run its course.

These necessary cessations often had an opportuneness to them, coming at a pause in a prayer, say, or, as today, at a moment of remembrance, just as year by year the coughing and wheezing ushered in the start of the grandest remembrance of all, the Two-Minute Silence. The unorchestrated pauses, though, were generally less weighty than that but were so repeatedly apposite as to have acquired an almost liturgical significance, the whirring of the cogs and the clanking of the wheels serving to charge the moment, as did the ringing of the bell at the elevation of the Host.

In matters of faith Father Jolliffe might be thought a bit of a noodle but however felicitous the pause in question even he didn't quite identify it as the voice of God. Still, if it was not God speaking, sometimes he felt the Almighty was at least clearing his throat, coughing meaningfully as a reminder of his presence. Father Jolliffe could see no harm in the practice of the presence of God being conflated with the sound of the passage of time, though there were also occasions when the clock's timely intervention irritated him, feeling that there was no need sometimes for the deity to draw attention to himself so obviously. It had something of St Peter and the cock crowing thrice about it, not an incident Father Jolliffe was particularly fond of as it showed Jesus up as a bit of an 'I told you so', which on the quiet the priest felt he sometimes was anyway.

Today, though, the intervention of the clock was useful in that it gave the congregation a moment or two to dwell on what they might want to say about Clive and perhaps as a consequence once 12 had struck people were not slow to respond.

A man was straightaway on his feet testifying to Clive's skill and good humour crewing in a transatlantic yacht race and another to his unsuspected abilities as a gourmet cook, testimonials greeted with incredulity in some sections of the congregation ('Clive?') but elsewhere without surprise. A woman said what a good gardener he was and how he had gone on to paint her kitchen, while someone from *Woman's Hour* described him as 'bright-eyed and bushy-tailed' and evidenced the large congregation as a testimony to Clive's genius for friendship, a genius incidentally that is generally posthumous and, like 'touching life at many points' (which Clive was also said to have done), is only found in obituaries. On the other hand, 'not suffering fools gladly', another staple of the obituary column, was not said, Clive having suffered fools as a matter of course as this was partly what he was paid for.

A Japanese gentleman now stood up and addressed the congregation in Japanese, a series of emphatic and seemingly impassioned declarations of which no one, even those lucky enough to speak Japanese, understood a word, as the acoustics of the church (designed by Inigo Jones) made it sound like overhearing an argument. Still, whether out of admiration for his boldness in speaking at all or to compensate him for being Japanese and therefore unintelligible, the congregation gave him a round of applause.

He bowed to every corner of the church then sat down, by which time there were already two more people on their feet wanting to have a word. Treacher began to think his estimate of Father Jolliffe to have been wrong. There was no firm hand here and as a woman behind him said, 'It's going on a bit,' the Archdeacon made another adverse note.

Happy to see it go on was a publisher, a portly and pretentious figure who had never met Clive but was there escorting one of his authors (as yet unennobled), a woman with several bestsellers under her belt but whose work had recently taken a feminist turn and who he feared might be looking for a publisher to match. Coming along to the service just as a chore he had been amazed at the level and variety of celebrity represented and, in the way of publishers, began to scent a book. As more and more of the congregation stood up and the reminiscences about Clive accumulated the publisher grew steadily more excited, occasionally clutching his companion's arm or, like Treacher (but not), scribbling notes on the back of his Order of Service. He saw the book as quick and easy to produce, a tape-recording job largely, a collage of interviews each no more than two or three paragraphs long—a book for people who preferred newspapers and which read like gossip while masquerading as sociology. 'A portrait of a generation'.

Her affection for Clive notwithstanding the novelist found it hard to reciprocate the publisher's enthusiasm, her own work never having generated a comparable degree of fervour. A woman would understand. As the publisher jotted down the names of possible writers she determined to take her next book where it would be better appreciated. She yawned.

Others were yawning too. Now an elderly couple

got up and left, followed a few minutes later by a younger man, tapping his watch, portraying helplessness and mouthing 'Sorry' to an unidentified friend in one of the pews behind.

FATHER JOLLIFFE WAS now wishing he'd never let the congregation off the leash. They were popping up all over the place, never fewer than two people on their feet waiting their turn. Some didn't stand but put a hand up, one of the most persistent a drab youth in an anorak sitting towards the front on the aisle. How he had come to know Clive Father Jolliffe could not imagine.

As a woman ended some protracted hymn to Clive's 'nurturing touch' Father Jolliffe managed to get in before the next speaker. 'I feel,' he said tentatively, 'that as time's getting on we ought to think about drawing these delightful reminiscences to a close,' a warning word that had the opposite effect to that intended as it galvanised all those who had not yet made up their minds to speak now to try and do so. In particular it made the drab youth start waving his hand as if he were still at school and trying to catch the teacher's eye. He looked as if he was at school, too, in jeans and blue anorak, though he had made some effort to dress up for the occasion by putting on a shirt and tie, the shirt rather too big at the collar and the cuffs almost covering his hands. Father Jolliffe wished he would be more forthright and not wait to be called but just stand up and get on with it like other people were doing, currently a philosopher, well groomed and bronzed from a sabbatical at Berkeley.

'Though we knew his name was Clive,' he was saying, 'we'—his wife sitting beside him smiled—'we called him Max, a name I came to feel suited him well. It's not entirely a nice name, not plain certainly or wholesome. In fact Max, really, is the name of a charmer, implying a degree of sophistication, a veneer of social accomplishment. It's urban, metropolitan, the name of someone who could take a vacant place at a poker game, say, and raise no eyebrows, which someone called . . . oh, Philip, say, couldn't.'

At this a woman in front turned round. 'I called him Philip.' Then turning to her neighbour. 'He said that was what he felt like inside.'

'I called him Bunny,' said a man on the aisle and this was the signal for other names to be tossed around—Toby, Alex and even Denis, all, however unlikely, attested to and personally guaranteed by various members of the congregation—so that still on his feet to bear witness to the unique appropriateness of Max the philosopher begins to feel a bit of a fool and says lamely, 'Well, he was always Max to us but this was obviously a many-sided man . . . which is yet another cause for celebration.' And sits down plumply to a re-assuring pat from his wife.

One of the names submitted in contention with Max was Betty, the claims for which had been quite belligerently advanced by a smallish young man in a black suit and shaven head who was sitting towards the front with several other young men similarly suited and shorn, one or two of them with sunglasses lodged on top of their hairless heads.

Now, ignoring the woman whose turn it was and the feebly waving youth, the young man, who gave his name as Carl, addressed the congregation. 'Knowing Clive well I think he would be touched if some-one'—he meant himself—'were to say something about him as a lover?'

A couple who had just got up to go straightaway sat down again. There was a hush, then a woman in the front row said: 'Excuse me. Before you do that I think we ought to see if this lady minds.' She indi-cated her neighbour, a shabby old woman in a bat-tered straw hat, her place also occupied by a couple of greasy shopping bags. 'She might mind. She is Mr Dunlop's aunt.'

Father Jolliffe closed his eyes in despair. It was Miss Wishart and she was not Clive's aunt at all. Well into her eighties and with nothing better to do Miss Wishart came to every funeral or memorial service that took place at the church, which was at least warm and where she could claim to be a distant relative of the deceased, a pretence not hard to maintain as she was genuinely hard of hearing and so could ignore the occasional probing question. Sometimes when she was lucky (and the relatives were stupid) she even got invited back for the funeral tea. All this Father Jolliffe knew and could have said, but it was already too late as Carl was even now sauntering round to the front pew where Miss Wishart was sitting in order to put the question to her directly.

With set face and making no concessions to her age or sensibilities Carl stood over Miss Wishart. 'Do you mind if we talk about your nephew's sex life?' Her neighbour repeated this in Miss Wishart's ear and while she considered the question, which she heard as having to do with his ex-wife, Carl looked up at Father Jolliffe. 'And you don't object, padre?'

It's often hard these days for the clergy not to think

of God as a little old-fashioned and Father Jolliffe was
no exception. So if he was going to object it wasn't
on grounds of taste or decorum but simply in order to
cut the service short. But what he really objected to
was the condescension of 'padre' (and even its hint of
a sneer) so this made him feel he couldn't object on
any grounds at all without the young man thinking he
was a ninny.

'No, I've no objection,' he said, 'except'—and he
looked boldly down at this small-headed creature—'I
think what we're talking about is love. Clive's love
life.' Then, thinking that didn't sound right either, 'His
life of love.'

That sounded even worse and the young man
smirked.

Treacher sighed. Jolliffe had been given an opportunity to put a stop to all this nonsense and he had muffed
it. Had he been in charge he would have put the young
man in his place, got the congregation on their knees
and the service would have been over in five minutes.
Now there was no telling what would happen.

As an indication that the proceedings were descend-
ing into chaos Treacher noted that one or two men in
the congregation now felt relaxed enough to take out

mobile phones and carry on hushed conversations, presumably rearranging appointments for which the length of the service was now making them late. The young man in front pocketed his cigarettes and lighter and strolled up the aisle to slip out of the West door where he found that two or three other likeminded smokers had preceded him. They nattered moodily in nicotine's enforced camaraderie before grinding their fags into the gravestones and rejoining the service at the point where the question about her nephew's sex life had at last got through to Miss Wishart and her neighbour was able to announce the verdict to the congregation. 'His aunt doesn't mind.'

There was a smattering of applause to signify approval of such exemplary open-mindedness in one so old, but since the question Miss Wishart thought she'd been asked was not to do with her nephew's sex life but with his next life, her tolerance hadn't really been put to the test.

'I JUST THOUGHT,' said Carl standing on the chancel steps, 'that it would be kind of nice to say what Clive was like in bed?' It was a question but not one that expected an answer. 'I mean, not in detail, obviously, only that he was good? He took his time and without being, you know, mechanical he was really inventive? I want,' he said, 'to take you on a journey? A journey round Clive's body?'

Treacher sank lower in his seat and Geoffrey's smile lost some of its benevolence as Carl did just that, dwelling on each part, genitals for the moment excepted, with the fervour if not quite the language of the metaphysical poets.

Though it was a body Geoffrey was at least acquainted with, Carl's version of it rang no bells and so he was reassured when he saw one or two in the congregation smiling wistfully and shaking their heads as if Carl had missed the point of Clive's body. Still, Geoffrey hoped nobody was going to feel strongly enough about this discrepancy to offer up a rival version as, however fascinating this material was, he felt there was a limit to what the congregation would stand.

'Do we really want to know this?' a senior official in the Foreign Office muttered to his wife (though in truth he knew some of it already and unbeknownst to him, so did she).

Actually Geoffrey was surprised at Carl's forbearance in omitting the penis, an intimate survey of which he was obviously capable of providing did he so choose.

Perhaps, Geoffrey thought, he was saving it up but if so it was to no purpose as it was while Carl was en route from the scrotum to the anus that suddenly it all got too much and a man was bold enough to shout out: 'Shame.'

Carl rounded on him fiercely. 'No, there was no shame. No shame then and no shame now. If you didn't understand that about Clive, you shouldn't be here.'

After which, though there were no more interruptions, the congregation felt slightly bullied and so took on a mildly mutinous air.

A woman sitting near to the front and quite close to Carl said almost conversationally: 'And you made this journey quite often, did you?'

'What journey?'

'Round Clive's body.'

'Sure. Why?'

'It's just that, while I may be making a fool of myself here,' and she looked round for support, 'I didn't know he was . . . that way.'

Several women who were within earshot nodded agreement.

'To me he was—' and she knew she was on dangerous ground, 'to me, he wasn't that way at all.'

Carl frowned. 'Do you mean gay?'

The woman (she was a buyer for Marks and Spencer's) smiled kindly and nodded.

'Well let me tell you,' said Carl, 'he was "that way".'

Though these exchanges are intimate and conversational they filter back through the congregation where they are greeted with varying degrees of astonishment, some of it audible.

'She didn't know?'

'Who's she kidding?'

'Clive,' the woman went on, 'never gave me to suppose that his sexual preferences were other than normal.'

'It is normal,' shouted Carl.

'I apologise. I mean conventional.'

'It's conventional, too.'

'Straight then,' said the buyer with a gesture of defeat. 'Let's say straight.'

'Say what you fucking like,' said Carl, 'only he wasn't. He was gay.'

Smiling and unconvinced she shook her head but said no more.

During this exchange Geoffrey had been thinking about Carl's hair or lack of it, the gleam of his skull through the blond stubble making him look not unlike a piglet. Once upon a time hair as short as this would have been a badge of a malignant disposition, a warning to keep clear, with long hair indicating a corresponding lenity. With its hint of social intransigence it had become a badge of sexual deviance, which it still seemed to be, though nowadays it was also a useful mask for incipient baldness, cutting the hair short a way of pre-empting the process.

'Fucking' had put a stop to these musings though Carl had said it so casually that for all they were in church no one seemed shocked (Treacher fortunately hadn't heard it) and Father Jolliffe decided to let it pass.

In his fencing match with the buyer from M&S Carl had undoubtedly come out on top but it had plainly disconcerted him and though he resumed his journey round Clive's body, when he got to his well-groomed armpits he decided to call it a day. 'When someone dies so young,' he summed up, 'the pity of it and the waste of it touch us all. But when he or she dies of Aids'—someone in the congregation gave a faint cry—'there should be anger as well as pity, and a resolve to fight this insidious disease and the prejudice it arouses and not to rest until we have a cure.' Carl sat down to be embraced by two of his friends, his stubbly head rubbed by a third.

. . .

HEARING AIDS MENTIONED for the first time and what had hitherto been vague fears and suspicions now given explicit corroboration many in the congregation found it hard to hide their concern, this death which had hitherto been an occasion for sorrow now a cause for alarm.

One woman sobbed openly, comforted by her (slightly pensive) husband.

A man knelt down and prayed, his companion stroking his back gently as he did so.

'I didn't think you needed to die of it any more,' a round the world yachtswoman whispered to her husband. 'I thought there were drugs.'

Others just sat there stunned, their own fate now prefigured, this memorial service a rehearsal for their own.

One of these, of course, was Father Jolliffe who is professional enough, though, to think this sobering down might be given prayerful expression, all this worry and concern channelled into an invocation not only for Clive but for all the victims of this frightful disease and not merely here but in Africa, Asia and America and so on. The landscape of the petition taking shape in his mind he stood up and faced the congregation. 'Shall we pray.'

As he himself knelt he saw the student-type in the anorak, impervious to the atmosphere obviously, still with his hand up and waving it even more vigorously now. But enough had been said and the priest ignored him.

There is a hush, with Treacher relieved that Father Jolliffe has at last got a grip on the service and is now going to bring these unseemly proceedings to a fitting conclusion.

'Vicar.'

It was the young man in the anorak. His voice was very clear in the silence and those of the congregation who had knelt or just put their heads down now raised them to look and Treacher, who had felt this service could hold no more surprises, said 'Oh God' and would have put his head in his hands had it not been there already.

Even the easy-going Father Jolliffe was taken aback at this unheard-of interruption. 'I was praying,' he said reproachfully.

He thought the young man blushed but he was looking so worked up it was hard to tell. A long-wristed, narrow-faced, straight-shouldered young man now looking sheepish. 'I did have my hand up before,' he said. 'And besides, it's probably relevant to the prayer.'

Had it not come at such an inopportune moment the notion that a prayer needed to be up to the minute and take account of all relevant information would have merited some thought and indeed might have provided a useful subject for 'Faith and Time', the series of discussion groups Father Jolliffe was currently running after Evensong on Sundays; the topicality of intercession in the light of the omniscience of God, for instance, or prayers taking place in time and God not. As it was the priest found himself staring at the young man, all pastoral feeling suspended, and saying rather crossly, 'Well?'

'My name is Hopkins,' said the young man. 'I'm on my year out. I'm going to do geology. I was in South America looking at rocks.'

Some of this he said loudly enough for the congregation to hear, but other less relevant remarks he gave almost as an aside to the nearby pews, so that somebody out of range said: 'What?'

'On his year out, doing geology,' somebody else called back.

'And?' said somebody else under their breath.

'I got sponsorship from Tilcon,' the young man added redundantly.

Somebody sighed heavily and said: 'Do we need to know this?'

'That was why I was in Peru. The rocks are very good there.'

'Can't hear,' said a well-known commentator on the arts. 'I know about Peru and even I can't hear.'

A woman nearby smiled kindly at the boy, and indicated he should speak up.

'The thing is'—and the speaking up made him sound defiant—'I was staying in the same hotel as Mr Dunlop when he died, and he didn't die of Aids.'

Finding him so unprepossessing and with no air of authority whatever (and, it has to be said, younger than most of their children) the congregation were disinclined to give him much attention. What had seemed just another tedious reminiscence is at first listlessly received and it's only when the glad message 'Not Aids' begins to be passed round and its significance realised that people begin to take notice, some at the back even standing up to get a better view of this unlikely herald.

It takes a little time and to begin with there is some shaking of heads but soon smiles begin to break out, people perk up and this nondescript young man suddenly finds himself addressing an audience that hangs on his every word. 'I know there is nothing to be ashamed of whatever it was he died of, but with all due respect to the person who spoke, who obviously knew him much better than I did, all the same I was there when he died and I'm sure his aunt, at least, would like to know it was not Aids.'

'HIV-related,' corrected a man with a ponytail.

'Yes, whatever,' says the student.

'It wasn't Aids,' Miss Wishart's helpful neighbour shouts in her ear. 'Not Aids.'

Meeting an uncomprehending smile from the old lady, she thinks to mime the condition by pointing to her bottom and shaking her head, thereby causing much offence to Carl and his glabrous colleagues and bringing Miss Wishart no nearer enlightenment. The only aids she has come across are deaf aids and hers plainly isn't working.

Hopkins, having given his welcome news, offers no evidence to back it up and now seems disposed to sit down again except that Father Jolliffe, who, if he had been an MP and addressing the House of Commons, would at this point have had to preface his question by declaring an interest, leans over the lectern and says, 'And do you mind telling us Mr . . . ?'

'Hopkins.'

'Mr Hopkins, do you mind telling us how Mr Dunlop did die?'

The young man blew his nose, carefully wiped it, and put away his handkerchief.

'Well, basically he had been on a trip which took him through some rough country where he was like bitten by some insect or other, you know, the name of which I can't remember, only the doctors at the hospital knew it. He got this fever. He was in the room next door to me at the hotel, to begin with anyway. Then they took him in and that was it basically. I was surprised as it's not a tropical place. The climate's not very different from Sheffield. I come from Sheffield,' he added apologetically.

Hopkins remained on his feet looking round at the congregation and smiling helpfully as if to suggest that if there were any more questions he would be happy to try and answer them. He doesn't have long to wait.

'I do not believe this,' Carl mutters as he gets to his feet though it is not to ask a question. He wholly ignores the student and talks to the church. 'I'm sorry? I thought we'd grown up? I thought we'd learned to look this thing in the face? I never thought I'd still be hearing tales of some ailment picked up in the wilds of Tibet. Or a wasting disease caught from the udders of Nepalese yaks. It's not from a bite. It's not from cat hairs. It's not from poppers nor is it a congenital disease of the dick. It's a virus passed via blood and sex and that's how it's caught. Not from some fucking Peruvian caterpillar. Of course it was Aids. Look at his life. How could it be anything else?'

In the silence that followed, many look desperately at the student in the hope he has something more to offer by way of rebuttal. But at 19 debate is hardly his strong point. He shrugs awkwardly and sits down shaking his head, long wrists dangling between his knees.

Unpleasant and arrogant though Carl had been, and with a manner seemingly designed to put people's backs up, there were many in the congregation who felt that he was right. They longed passionately to believe in this Peruvian caterpillar and its death-dealing bite. South America was a dangerous place, everyone knew that; there were the pampas, gauchos and regular revolutions. The Maya had perished, so why not Clive? But what Carl had said made sense. Of course it was Aids. No one could screw as much as he had done and go unpunished. So the sentence that had been all too briefly remitted was now reimposed and hopes momentarily raised were dashed once more. But to have been given a vision of peace of mind and then to see it snatched away made the burden even harder to bear.

One couple held each other's hands in mute misery. Which had slept with Clive—or both? What did it matter? Never had they been so close.

Still, the couples who had shared Clive's favours were better placed than husbands or wives who had known him singly. 'What does it signify anyway,' said a fierce-eyebrowed judge, who knew Clive only as someone who occasionally unfroze his shoulder. 'He's dead, that's the essence of it.' His wife, who was keeping very quiet, shifted in her seat slightly as she was suffering from thrush, or that was what she hoped.

Symptoms were back generally. A pitiless quiz-show host found herself with a dry mouth. The suffragan bishop knew he had a rash. A stand-up comedian had a cold sore that didn't seem to clear up and which was masked by make-up. Now it had suddenly begun to itch. He had a powder compact but dared not consult it. Those who were famous, though, knew better than to turn a hair. Their anxiety must be kept private and unshown for they were always under scrutiny. They must wait to share their worries discreetly with friends or, if with the general public, at a decent price from the newspapers concerned.

Husbands who thought their wives didn't know, put a face on it (though their wives did know very often). Wives who thought their husbands didn't know (which they generally didn't) masked their distraction in a show of concern for others, one, for instance, patting the shoulder of a man in front who, without looking, took the hand and held it to his cheek.

The congregation had been given a glimpse of peace; the itch had gone, the cough had stilled, the linen was unsoiled; the pores had closed, the pus dried up and the stream ran clear and cool. But that was what it had been, a glimpse only. Now there was to be no healing. There was only faith.

How to put this into prayer. Father Jolliffe clasped his hands and tried once more. 'Shall we pray?'

They settled and waited as he sought for the words.

'May I speak?'

Baulked for a second unbelievable time on the brink of intercession, Father Jolliffe nearly said 'No' (which is what the Archdeacon would have said, who has long since written down: 'Hopeless. Lacks grip.' And now inserts 'totally').

Father Jolliffe searches the congregation to see who it is who has spoken and sees, standing at the back, a tall, distinguished-looking man. 'I am a doctor,' he says.

This is unsurprising because it is just what he looks like. He is dry, kindly-faced and yet another one who doesn't speak up. 'I am a doctor,' he repeats. 'Mr Dunlop's doctor, in fact. While his medical history must, of course, be confidential'—'Must be what?' somebody says. 'Controversial,' says someone else—'I think I am not breaking any rules when I say that Mr Dunlop was a most . . . ah . . . responsible patient and came to me over a period of years for regular blood tests.'

'Regular blood tests,' goes round the pews.

'These were generally a propos HIV, the last one only a week before his departure for South America. It was negative. What this fever was that he died of I'm in no position to say, but contrary to the assertions made by the gentleman who spoke earlier'—he meant Carl—'it seems to me most unlikely, in fact virtually impossible, that it was HIV-related. Still,' he smiled sadly, 'the fact remains that Clive is dead and I can only offer my condolences to his grieving friends and to his aunt. Whatever it was her nephew died of, her grief must be unchanged.'

Miss Wishart is nudged by her neighbour and when

the doctor is pointed out to her, smiles happily and gives him a little wave. She seldom got such a good ride as this.

As the doctor sat down there was a ripple of applause and as the news filtered to the acoustically disadvantaged areas of the church it grew and grew. People at the front stood up and began applauding louder and those further back followed suit until the whole church was on its feet clapping.

'Good old Clive!' someone shouted.

'Trust Clive,' said someone else and there was even some of that overhead clapping and wild whoops that nowadays characterises audiences in a TV studio or at a fashionable first night.

Seldom even at a wedding had the vicar seen so many happy faces, some openly laughing, some weeping even and many of them embracing one another as they were called on to do in the Communion Service, but never with a fervour or a fellow-feeling so unembarrassed as this. It was, thought Father Jolliffe, just as it should be.

Still, it was hard to say what it was they were applauding: Clive for having died of the right thing (or not having died of the wrong one) and for having been so sensible about his blood tests; the young student for having brought home the news; or the urbane-looking doctor for having confirmed it. Father Jolliffe was glad to see that God came in for some of the credit and mindful of the setting one woman sank to her knees in prayer, and both genders got onto their mobiles to relay the news to partners and friends whose concern for themselves (and for Clive, of course) was as keen as those present in the congregation.

Some wept and, seeing the tears, wondering partners took them as tears for Clive. But funeral tears seldom flow for anyone other than the person crying them and so it was here. They cried for Clive, it is true, but they cried for themselves without Clive, particularly now that his clean and uncomplicated death meant that he had thankfully left them with nothing to remember him by.

Amid the general rejoicing even Carl looked a little more cheerful, though it was hard for him to be altogether wholehearted, the dead man just having been dropped from a club of which Carl was still a life member and from which he stood no chance of exclusion. There were one or two others in the same boat and knew it, but they clapped too, and tried to rejoice.

Though his companion the novelist was gratefully weeping, the publisher's thanksgiving was less wholehearted. Aids never did sales any harm and gave a tragic momentum even to the silliest of lives, whereas it was hard not to think that there was only bathos in a death that resulted from being bitten by a caterpillar. Still, the geology student seemed naive and possibly suggestible, so Clive's death could be made—and moralistically speaking ought to be made—more ambiguous than it really was. Nobody liked someone who had had as much sex as Clive to get off scot free and that included the idle reader. No, there was a book here even so; the absurd death was just a hiccup and smiling too, the publisher joined in the clapping.

But clapping whom? Father Jolliffe decided it might as well be God and raising his voice above the tumult he said: 'Now (and for the third time of asking), shall we pray?' This even got a laugh and there was a last whoop before the congregation settled down. 'Let us in the silence remember our friend Clive, who is dead but is alive again.'

This, however hallowed, was not just a phrase. Clive's imagined death had been baneful and fraught with far-reaching implications so that, devoid of these, his real (and more salubrious) demise did seem almost a resurrection. And in that cumbrous silence, laden with prayers unmouthed, loosed from anxiety and re-crimination many do now try and remember him, some frowning as they pray with eyes closed but seeing him still, some open-eyed but unseeing of the present, lost in recollection. In the nature of things, these memories are often inappropriate. Some think, for instance, of what Clive felt like, smelled like, recalling his tenderness and his tact. There was the diligence of his application and pictured in more than one mind's eye was that stern and labouring face rising and falling in the conscientious performance of his professional duties.

'I sing his body,' prayed Geoffrey to himself. 'I sing his marble back, his heavy legs'—he had been reading Whitman—'I sing the absence of preliminaries, the curtness of desire. Dead, but not ominously so, now I extol him.'

'I elevate him,' thought a choreographer (for whom he had also made some shelves), 'a son of Job dancing before the Lord.'

'I dine him,' prayed one of the cooks, 'on quails stuffed with pears in a redcurrant coulis.'

'I adorn him,' imagined a fashion designer. 'I send him down the catwalk in chest-revealing tartan tunic and trews and sporting a tam o'shanter.'

'I appropriate him,' planned the publisher, 'a young man eaten alive by celebrity' (the dust-jacket Prometheus on the rock).

None, though, thought of words and how the bedroom had been Clive's education. It was there that he learned that words mattered, once having been in bed with an etymologist whose ejaculation had been indefinitely postponed when Clive (on being asked if he was about to come too) had murmured, 'Hopefully.' In lieu of discharge, the etymologist had poured his frustrated energy into a short lecture on neologisms which Clive had taken so much to heart he had never said 'hopefully' again.

Nothing surprised him, nothing shocked him. He was not—the word nowadays would be judgmental, but Clive knew that there were some who disliked this word, too, and preferred censorious, but he was not judgmental of that either.

Words mattered and so did names. He knew if someone disliked their name and did not want it said, still less called out, during lovemaking. He knew, too, his clients' various names for the private parts and what he or she preferred to call them and what they preferred him to call them (which was not always the same thing). He knew, too, in the heightened atmosphere of the bedroom how swiftly a misappellation in this regard could puncture desire and shrivel its manifestation.

He brought to the bedroom a power of recall and a grasp of detail that would have taken him to the top of any profession he had chosen to enter. A man who could after several months' interval recall which breast his client preferred caressed could have run the National Theatre or reformed the Stock Exchange. He knew what stories to whisper and when not to tell stories at all and knew, too, when the business was over, never to make reference to what had been said.

Put simply this was a man who had learned never to strike a false note. He was a professional.

Aloud Geoffrey said: 'Let us magnify him before the Lord. O all ye works of the Lord, bless ye the Lord: praise him and magnify him for ever.'

Geoffrey rose to his feet. 'And now we end this service of thanksgiving with John Keble's hymn.'

New every morning is the love . . .
Our waking and uprising prove
Through sleep and darkness safely brought
Restored to life and power and thought.

How glumly they had come into the church and how happily now, their burden laid down, do they prepare to go forth. So they sing this mild little hymn as the chorus sings their deliverance in *Fidelio*, or the crowd sings at Elland Road. They sing, distasteful though that spectacle often is, as they sing at the Last Night of the Proms. And singing they are full of new resolve.

Since the news of Clive's death a shadow had fallen across sexual intercourse. Coming together had become wary, the whole business perfunctory and self-serving, and even new relationships had been entered on gingerly. As one wife, not in the know, had complained, 'There is no giving any more.' In some bedrooms where intercourse had not been wholly discontinued prophylactics had appeared for the first time, variously explained by a trivial infection or a sudden sensitivity, but in all cases made out to the unknowing partner as just a minor precaution not the membrane between life and death.

Now that time of sexual austerity was over. This was the liberation, and many of the couples pressing out of the door looked forward to resuming all those sexually sophisticated manoeuvres that Clive's death and its presumed cause had seen discontinued.

Partners not in the know were taken aback by the gusto with which their long-diffident opposites now went to it, and some, to put it plainly, could scarcely wait to get home in order to have a fuck. And indeed some didn't, one couple sneaking round behind the church to the alcove outside the vestry that sheltered the dustbins and doing it there. They happened both to be friends of Clive and so of the same mind, but several husbands, ignorant of their wives' connection with the dead man, were startled to find themselves unexpectedly fingered and fondled (evidence of the strong tide of relief that was sweeping their partners along) and one, made to park on a double yellow line in the Goswell Road, had to spread a copy of the *Financial Times* over his knees while beneath it his wife gave vent to her euphoria.

For some, though, deliverance would be all too brief. A TV designer, a particular friend of Clive and thus feeling himself more enshadowed than most, was so rapturous at the news of Clive's unportentous death that he celebrated by picking up a dubious young man in Covent Garden, spending a delightful evening and an unprotected night, waking the next morning as anxious as he had been before and in much the same boat.

Still, others thought they had learned their lesson

and crowding up the aisles they saw the west door open on a churchyard now bathed in sunlight. The bells were ringing out; the vicar was there shaking hands; truly this had been a thanksgiving and an ending and now the portals were flung open on a new life.

'I presume he had us all on his computer some- where,' someone said.

'Who cares?' said someone else.

Slowly they shuffled towards the light.

IT WAS NOW well past lunchtime and the Archdeacon had stomach ache. Anxious to get away before the crowd and unobserved by the vicar, who would surely be shaking all those famous hands, Canon Treacher had got up smartly after the blessing only to find his exit from the pew blocked by a woman doing what she (and Canon Treacher) had been brought up to do, namely, on entering or leaving a church to say a private prayer. It was all Treacher could do not to step over her, but instead waited there fuming while she placidly prayed. She took her time with God, and then, her devotions ended, more time assembling her umbrella, gloves and what she called apologetically 'my bits and bobs' and then when she was finally ready, had to turn back to retrieve her Order of Service, which she held up at Canon Treacher with a brave smile as if to signify that this had been a job well done. By which time, of course, the aisle was clogged with people and Treacher found himself carried slowly but inexorably towards the door where, as he had feared, Father Jolliffe was now busy shaking hands.

Even so, the priest was so deep in conversation with a leading chat-show host that Treacher thought he was going to manage to sidle by unnoticed. Except that then the priest saw him and the chat-show host, used to calling the shots with regard to when conversations began and ended, was startled to find this chat abruptly wound up as Jolliffe hastened across to shake Treacher's cold, withdrawing hand.

'Archdeacon. What a pleasure to see you. Did you know Clive?'

'Who? Certainly not. How should I know him?'

'He touched life at many points.'

It was a joke but Treacher did not smile.

'Not at this one.'

'And did you enjoy the service?' Father Jolliffe's plump face was full of pathetic hope.

Treacher smiled thinly but did not yield. 'It was . . . interesting.'

With Father Jolliffe cringing under the archidiaconal

disapproval it ought to have been a chilling moment and, by Treacher at least, savoured and briefly enjoyed, but it was muffed when the hostess of a rapid response TV cookery show, whom the vicar did not know, suddenly flung her arms round his neck saying, 'Oh, pumpkin!'

Firm in the culinary grasp, Father Jolliffe gazed helplessly as the Archdeacon was borne away on the slow-moving tide and out into the chattering churchyard where, holy ground notwithstanding, Treacher noted that many of the congregation were already feverishly lighting up.

When, a few days later, Treacher delivered his report, it was not favourable, which saddened the Bishop (who had, though it's of no relevance, been a great hurdler in his day). Rather mischievously he asked Treacher if he had nevertheless managed to enjoy the service.

'I thought it,' said Treacher, 'a useful lesson in the necessity for ritual. Or at any rate, form. Ritual is a road, a path between hedges, a track along which the priest leads his congregation.'

'Yes,' said the Bishop, who had been here before.

'Leave the gate open, nay tell them it's open as this

foolish young man did, and straightaway they're through it, trampling everything underfoot.'

'You make the congregation sound like cattle, Arthur.'

'No, not cattle, Bishop. Sheep, a metaphor for which there is some well-known authority in scripture. It was a scrum. A free-for-all.'

'Yes,' said the Bishop. 'Still,' he smiled wistfully, 'That gardening girl, the footballer who's always so polite—I quite wish I'd been there.'

Treacher, feeling unwell, now passes out of this narrative, though with more sympathy and indeed regret than his acerbities might seem to warrant. Though he had disapproved of the memorial service and its altogether too heartfelt antics he is not entirely to be deplored, standing in this tale for dignity, formality and self-restraint.

Less feeling was what Treacher wanted, the services of the church, as he saw it, a refuge from the prevailing sloppiness. As opportunities multiplied for the display of sentiment in public and on television—confessing, grieving and giving way to anger, and always with a ready access to tears—so it seemed to Treacher that there was needed a place for dryness and self-control and this was the church. It was not a popular view and he sometimes felt that he had much in common with a Jesuit priest on the run in Elizabethan England—clandestine, subversive and holding to the old faith, even though the tenets of that faith, discretion, understatement and respect for tradition, might seem more suited to tailoring than they did to religion.

Once out of the churchyard the Archdeacon lit up, his smoking further evidence that there was more to this man than has been told in this tale. There had briefly been a Mrs Treacher, a nice woman but she had died. He would die soon, too, and the Bishop at least would be relieved.

BACK AT THE CHURCH, Geoffrey was shaking hands to the finish, with last out, as always, Miss Wishart who was still attesting her supposed connection with the deceased. 'Somebody said something about drinks for my nephew. Where would they be? A sherry was what he preferred only I like wine.'

The priest pointed her vaguely in the direction of the churchyard which with people standing about talking and laughing looked like a cocktail party anyway. He had been asked to drinks himself by a florid and effusive character, a publisher apparently, with a stony-faced woman in tow. He had taken both Geoffrey's hands warmly in his, saying he had this brilliant idea for a book and he wanted to run it past him.

This, taken with the upbeat conclusion of the service, ought to have cheered him, but Father Jolliffe found himself despondent. The presence of the Archdeacon could only mean one thing: he had been vetted. For what he wasn't sure, but for promotion certainly. And equally certainly he had failed to impress. For a start he should not have invited the congregation to participate. He knew that from something that had happened at the Board, when in answer to a question about the kiss of peace and the degree of conviviality acceptable at the Eucharist, he had said that the priest was, in a real sense, the master of ceremonies. This had got a laugh from the Board (the Bishop actually guffawing), except that he had noticed that Treacher was smiling in a different way and making one of his spidery notes: he was not impressed then and he had not been impressed now.

Still had he not, as it were, thrown the service open to the floor, the true circumstances of Clive's death would never have emerged so he could not regret that.

What the Lord giveth the Lord also taketh away. He went back into the now empty church to get out of his gear.

'SHOULD I HAVE SPOKEN?' Hopkins was still slumped in his pew. Now he got up clutching his backpack in front of him like a shield. 'I wondered if it was out of turn.'

'Not at all,' said Geoffrey, noticing that the young man had loosened the unaccustomed tie and undone the top button of his shirt, so that he looked younger still and not so old-fashioned. It was difficult to think of him at Clive's death-bed.

'You did the right thing, Mr Hopkins. There were many people'—he didn't say himself—'who were grateful. It lifted a burden.'

The boy sat down again cradling his backpack. 'The young guy seemed pretty pissed off. The—' he hesitated, 'the gay one?'

Hopkins had an unconvincing earring that Geoffrey had not spotted, ear and earring now briefly caught in a shaft of light, a faint fuzz on the fresh pink ear.

'People were upset,' Geoffrey said. 'Clive was . . . well, Clive.' He smiled, but the young man still looked unhappy.

'I felt a fool.' He sat hugging his backpack then suddenly brightened up. 'That blonde from *EastEnders* was on my row. Clive never told me he knew her.'

Geoffrey thought that there were probably quite a few things Clive had never told him and wondered if anything had happened between them. Probably not, if only because he imagined there was more on offer in South America and the local talent doubtless more exotic.

He was an awkward boy with big hands. He was the kind of youth Modigliani painted and for a moment Geoffrey wondered if he was attractive, but decided he was just young.

'And that cook who slags people off? He was here too.'

'Yes,' said Geoffrey. 'It was a good turn-out.' Then, feeling he ought to be getting on. 'They're all outside.'

The youth did not notice the hint still less take it. 'You said you knew Clive?'

'Yes,' said Geoffrey, then added, 'but not well.'

'I'd never seen anybody die before. It was depressing?'

Geoffrey smiled sadly and nodded as if this were an aspect of death that had not occurred to him. The youth was a fool.

'Can I show you something?' The student rooted in his pack then put it on the floor so that the priest could sit beside him. 'I had to go through his stuff after he died. There wasn't much. He was travelling light. Only there was this.'

It was a maroon notebook, long, cloth-covered and meant to fit easily into a pocket. Geoffrey thought he remembered it and ran his hand over the smooth, soft cover.

'Is it a diary?' the priest said.

'Not exactly.'

IN THE CHURCHYARD the party was beginning to break up. One group had arranged to lunch at the Garrick and were moving round saying their farewells while someone looked for a cab. Others were going off to investigate a new restaurant that had opened in a converted public lavatory and of which they'd heard good reports, though tempted to join forces with yet another party who were venturing into one of the last genuine cafés patronised by the porters at Smithfield where the tripe was said to be delicious.

Most of the big stars had left pretty promptly, their cars handily waiting nearby to shield them from too much unmediated attention. The pop star's limo dropped him first then called at the bank so that the security guard could redeposit the clasp and then took him on to a laboratory in Hounslow where, as a change from Catherine the Great, he was mounting vigil over some hamsters testing lip-gloss. Meanwhile, the autograph hunters moved among what was left of the congregation, picking up what dregs of celebrity that remained.

'Are you anybody?' a woman said to the partner of a soap-star, 'or are you just with him?'

'He was my nephew,' said Miss Wishart to anyone who would listen.

'Who, dear?' said one of the photographers, which of course Miss Wishart didn't hear, but she looked so forlorn he took her picture anyway, which was fortunate, as he was later able to submit it to the National Portrait Gallery where it duly featured in an exhibition alongside the stage doorman of the Haymarket and the maître d' of the Ivy as one of 'The Faces of London'.

Soon, though, it began to spit with rain and within a few minutes the churchyard was empty and after its brief bout of celebrity, back to looking as dingy and desolate as it generally did.

'No, it isn't a diary,' said Hopkins. 'It's more of an account book.'

It was divided into columns across the page, each

column numbered, possibly indicating a week or a month, the broad left-hand column a list of initials, and in the other columns figures, possibly amounts. The figures were closely packed and as neat as the work of a professional accountant.

'Can you make it out?' said the young man, running his finger down the left-hand column. 'These are people, I take it.'

'They might be,' said Geoffrey. 'I don't quite know.' Having just spotted his own initials, Geoffrey knew only too well, though he noted that the spaces opposite his own name were only occasionally filled in. This was because Clive came round quite spasmodically and wasn't often available when Geoffrey called (now, seeing the number of people on his list, he could see why). When he did come round the visit did not always involve sex ('No funny business' is how Clive put it). Geoffrey told himself that this was because he was a clergyman and that he thus enjoyed a relationship with Clive that was pastoral as well as physical. More often than not this meant he found himself making Clive scrambled eggs, while Clive lay on the sofa watching TV in his underpants, which was about as close to domesticity as Geoffrey ever got. Still, Geoffrey had always insisted on paying for this privilege (hence the entries in the notebook), though really in order to give credence to the fiction that sex wasn't what their friendship was about. Though, since he was paying for it, it wasn't about friendship either, but that managed to be overlooked.

'Did you see a lot of each other? In Peru?'

Geoffrey was anxious to turn the page and get away from those incriminating initials.

'Yes. We had meals together quite often. I could never figure out what he was doing there.'

'What did you eat?' said Geoffrey. 'Eggs?'

'Beans, mostly. He said he was travelling round. Seeing the world.'

As casually as he could Geoffrey turned the page.

'These figures,' said Hopkins, turning it back. 'What do you think they mean?'

'They're on this page, too,' said Geoffrey turning the page again. 'And here,' turning another.

Hopkins blew his nose, wiped it carefully and put the handkerchief away. 'Is it sex, do you think?'

'Sex?' said Geoffrey with apparent surprise. 'Why should it be sex?' He looked at Hopkins as if the in-sinuation were his and almost felt sorry for him when the young geologist blushed.

'Clive was a masseur. They may be payments on

account—if they're payments at all. I think when he was hard up at one period he used to provide home help, carpentry and so on. It could be that.'

'Yes? You say he was a masseur. He told me he was a writer.'

Geoffrey smiled and shook his head.

'My guess is that it's a sort of diary and I don't feel,' Geoffrey said pompously, 'that one ought to read other people's diaries, do you?'

Hopkins shrank still further and Geoffrey hated himself. He went on leafing through. Against some of the names were small hieroglyphics that seemed to denote a sexual preference or practice, an indication of a client's predilections possibly, of which one or two were obvious. Lips with a line through, for instance, must mean the person with the initials didn't like being kissed; lips with a tick the reverse. But what did a drawing of a foot indicate? Or an ear? Or (in one case) two ears?

None of the drawings was in any sense obscene and were so small and symbolic as to be uninteresting in themselves, but what they stood for—with sometimes a line-up of three or four symbols in a row—was both puzzling and intriguing.

It was a shock, therefore, for Geoffrey to turn the

page and come across a note *en clair* that was both direct and naive:

> *Palaces I have done it in:*
> *Westminster*
> *Lambeth*
> *Blenheim*
> *Buckingham (2)*
> *Windsor*

Except Windsor was crossed out with a note, 'Not a palace' and an arrow led from Westminster to a bubble saying 'Lost count'. Written down baldly like this it seemed so childish and unsophisticated as not to be like Clive at all, though as notes for a book, Geoffrey could see it made some sort of sense.

'It's rather sad, really,' Geoffrey went on, still in his pompous mode. 'Why bother to write it down? Who'd be interested?'

'Oh, I keep notes myself,' said Hopkins. Then, as the priest looked up, startled, 'Oh, not about that. Just on rocks and stuff. He told me he was writing a book, but people do say that, don't they? Particularly in South America.'

It's true Clive had spoken of writing a book, or at

least of being able to write a book, 'I could write a book,' often how he ended an account of some outrageous escapade. Geoffrey may even have said, 'Why don't you?' though without ever dreaming he would.

Like many who hankered after art, though, Clive was saving it up, if not quite for a rainy day at least until the right opportunity presented itself—prison perhaps, a long illness or a spell in the back of beyond. Which, of course, Peru was and which was why, Geoffrey presumed, he had taken along the book.

Still, he wasn't sure. Clive was always so discreet and even when telling some sexual tale he seldom mentioned names and certainly not the kind of names represented at the memorial service. This iron discretion was, Clive knew, one of his selling points and part of his credit, so not an asset he was likely to squander. Or not yet anyway.

Hopkins seemed to be taking less interest in the diary and when Geoffrey closed the book and put it on the pew between them the young man did not pick it up but just sat staring into space.

Then: 'Of course, if it is sex and those are initials and you could identify them it would be dynamite.'

'Well, a mild sort of dynamite,' said Geoffrey, 'and

only if a person,' Geoffrey smiled at the young man, 'only if a person was planning to reveal information . . .' He left the sentence unfinished. 'And that would, of course, be . . .' and he left this sentence unfinished too, except at that moment a police car blared past outside. Geoffrey sighed. God could be so unsubtle sometimes. 'Besides,' he went on, 'if this is entirely about sex, and I'm not sure it is, it's not against the law is it?' He wondered how long he could get away with reckoning to be so stupid.

Having found someone, as he thought, more ingenuous than himself the young man was determined to instruct him in the ways of the world. 'No,' he said patiently, 'but it would make a story. Several stories probably. Stories for which newspapers would pay a lot of money.'

'You wouldn't do that, surely?'

'I wouldn't, but someone might.' Hopkins picked up the book. 'I wondered about handing it over to the police.'

'The police?' Geoffrey found himself suddenly angry at the boy's foolishness. 'What for?'

'For safe-keeping?'

'Safe-keeping,' shouted Geoffrey, all pretence of

naivety gone. 'Safe-keeping? In which case why bother with the police at all. Just cut out the middleman and give it to the *News of the World*?'

Taken aback by this unexpected outburst Hopkins looked even more unhappy. 'I don't know,' he said, nuzzling his chin on top of his pack. 'I just want to do the right thing.'

The right thing to do was nothing but Geoffrey did not say so. Instead he thought of all the people behind the initials, the troubled novelists, the tearful gardeners and stone-faced soap-stars, Clive's celebrity clientele dragged one by one into the sneering, pitiless light. Something had to be done.

He put his hand on the young man's knee.

He felt Hopkins flinch but kept his hand where he had put it, or not where he had put it, he decided subsequently, but where God had put it. Because tame and timid though such a move might seem (and to some-one of Clive's sophistication, for instance, nonchalant and almost instinctive), for Geoffrey it was momentous, fraught with risk and the dread of embarrassment. He had never made such a bold gesture in his life and now he had done it without thinking and almost without feeling.

The young man was unprepossessing and altogether

too awkward and angular; in the street he would not have looked at him twice. But there was his hand on the boy's knee. 'What is your name?' he said.

'Greg,' Hopkins said faintly. 'It's Greg.'

Geoffrey had no thought that the presence of his hand on the young man's knee would be the slightest bit welcome nor, judging by the look of panic on his face, was it. Greg was transfixed.

'I am wondering, Greg,' said Geoffrey, 'if we are getting this right. We are talking about what to do with this notebook when strictly speaking, *legally* speaking'— he squeezed the knee slightly—'it has got nothing to do with us anyway.'

'No?'

'No. The notebook belongs after all, to Clive. And now to his estate. And whom does his estate belong to . . . or will do eventually?'

Hopkins shook his head.

'His only surviving relative. Miss Wishart!'

The priest loosened his grip on the knee, though lingering there for a moment as it might be preparatory to travelling further up the young man's leg. This galvanised Hopkins and he got up suddenly. Except that the priest got up too, both crammed together in the close confinement of the pew, the priest seemingly unperturbed and never leaving his face his kind, professional, priestly smile.

Hopkins was now unwise enough to put his hand on the edge of the pew. Geoffrey promptly put his hand on top of it.

'No, no,' said Hopkins.

'No what?' said Geoffrey kindly.

'No, she should keep the book.' Hopkins pulled his hand away in order to retrieve the book still lying on the seat. 'Where can I find her?'

'She comes to church. I can give it to her.' Geoffrey reached for the book and fearful that he was reaching for him too, Hopkins relinquished it without a struggle.

'I can give it to her as a relic of her nephew. The only relic really.' He stroked the book fondly and in that instant Hopkins was out of the pew and on his way to the door. But not quickly enough to avoid the priest's kindly hand pressing into the small of his back and carrying with it the awful possibility that it might move lower down.

'Yes,' Hopkins said, 'give it to her. She's the person.' And stopping suddenly in order to put on his backpack he got rid of the hand, but then found it resting even more horribly on his midriff, so that he gave a hoarse involuntary cry before the priest lifted his hand with a bland smile, converting the gesture almost into a benediction.

'Won't she be shocked?' Hopkins said as he settled the pack on his back. 'She's an old lady.'

'No,' said Geoffrey firmly. 'And I say this, Greg, as her parish priest. It's true she's an old person but I have found the old are quite hard to shock. It's the young one has to be careful with. They are the prudes nowadays.'

Hopkins nodded. Irony and geology obviously did not mix.

'I wondered if you wanted a cup of tea?' Geoffrey stroked the side of his backpack.

'No,' he said hurriedly. 'No, I've got to be somewhere.'

Still widely smiling Geoffrey put out his hand.

They shook hands and the young man dashed out of the door and quickly across the wet gravestones, Geoffrey noting as he did so that he had that overlong and slightly bouncy stride he had always associated with flute-players, train-spotters and other such unworldly and unattractive creatures.

Something strange, though, now happened that Geoffrey would later come to see as prophetic. Or at least ominous. The boy had pulled out a knitted cap and as he stopped to put it on he saw the priest still standing there. Suddenly and unexpectedly the boy smiled and raised his hand. 'I'm sorry,' he called out, and then about to go, he stopped again. 'But thank you all the same.'

Geoffrey sat down in the nearest pew. He was trembling. After a bit he got up and went into the vestry where he opened the safe in which was kept the parish plate, the chalice (Schofield of London, 1782) and the two patens (Forbes of Bristol, 1718), each in its velvet-lined case. On the shelf below them Geoffrey put Clive's book.

OVER THE FOLLOWING WEEKS Geoffrey would often open up the safe and take a peek at the book, trying to decipher Clive's cryptography and gauge the extent and nature of his activities. None of it shocked him: indeed he found the exercise vaguely exciting and as near to pornography as he allowed himself to come.

Whether it was thanks to the book or to that almost involuntary pass that had allowed him to retain it Geoffrey found his life changing. Disappointed of immediate promotion he was now more . . . well, relaxed and though 'Relax!' is hardly at the core of the Christian message he did feel himself better for it.

So it might be because he was easier with himself or that his unique pass at the geology student had broken his duck and given him more nerve but one way and another he found himself having the occasional fling, in particular with the bus-driving crucifer, who, married though he was, didn't see that as a problem. Nor did Geoffrey's confessor who, while absolving him of what sin there was, urged him to see this and any similar experiences less as deviations from the straight and narrow and more as part of a learning curve. In fairness, this wasn't an expression Geoffrey much cared for, though he didn't demur. He preferred to think of it, if only to himself, as grace.

He still kept the book in the safe, though, as it represented a valorous life he would have liked to lead and still found exciting. It happened that he had been to confession the day before and just as a diabetic whose blood tests have been encouraging sneaks a forbidden pastry so he felt he deserved a treat and went along to the church meaning to take out Clive's book. It was partly to revisit his memory but also because even though he now knew its mysterious notations by heart they still gave him a faint erotic thrill. He knew that this was pathetic and could have told it to no one, except perhaps Clive, and it was one of the ways he missed him.

Pushing open the door of the church he saw someone sitting towards the front and on the side. It was the geology student, slumped in the same pew he had sat in at the memorial service.

'Hail,' said the young man. 'We meet again.' Geoffrey shook hands.

'I meant to come before now,' he said, 'only my car's not been well.'

Geoffrey managed a smile. Seeing him again, Geoffrey thought how fortunate it was that his advance had been rejected. God had been kind. It would never have done.

Hopkins made room for Geoffrey to sit down, just as he had on the first occasion they had talked.

'I came back,' he said, as if it were only that morning he had fled the church. 'I thought about it and I thought, why not?' And now he turned towards Geoffrey and looking him sternly in the eye put his hand on the vicar's knee. 'All right?'

Geoffrey did not speak.

There was a click, then another and the turning of a wheel and faintly, as if from a great way off, Geoffrey heard the cogs begin to grind as the clock gathered itself up and struck the hour.

Miss Fozzard

Finds Her Feet

Bit of a bombshell today. I'm just pegging up my stocking when Mr Suddaby says, 'I'm afraid, Miss Fozzard, this is going to have to be our last encounter.' Apparently this latest burglary has put the tin hat on things and what with Mrs Suddaby's mother finally going into a home and their TV reception always being so poor there's not much to keep them in Leeds so they're making a bolt for it and heading off to Scarborough. Added to which Tina, their chow, has a touch of arthritis so the sands may help and the upshot is they've gone in for a little semi near Peasholme Park.

'But,' Mr Suddaby says, 'none of that is of any consequence. What is important, Miss Fozzard, is what are we going to do about your feet? You've been coming to me for so long I don't like to think of your feet falling into the wrong hands.'

I said, 'Well, Mr Suddaby, I shall count myself very

lucky if I find someone as accomplished as yourself and, if I may say so, with your sense of humour.' Because it's very seldom we have a session in which laughter doesn't figure somewhere.

He said, 'Well, Miss Fozzard, chiropody is a small world and I've taken the liberty of making a few phone calls and come up with two possibilities. One is a young lady over in Roundhay, who, I understand is very reasonable.'

'A woman?' I said, 'In chiropody? Isn't that unusual?' 'No,' he said, 'not nowadays. The barriers are coming down in chiropody as in everything else. It's progress Miss Fozzard, the march of, and Cindy Bickerton has her own salon.' I said, 'Cindy? That doesn't inspire confidence. She sounds as if she should be painting nails not cutting them.'

'Well,' he said, 'in that case the alternative might be more up your street. I don't know him personally but Mr Dunderdale has got all the right letters after his name. He's actually retired but he still likes to take on a few selected clients, just to keep his hand in. However he does live out at Lawnswood and unless I'm very much mistaken you're not motorised?' I said, 'No problem. I can just bob on the 17. It's a bus I like. No, if it's all the same to you and the Equal Opportunities Board I'll opt for Mr Dunderdale.' He said, 'I think it's a wise decision. Allow me,' (and he winked) 'Allow me,' he said, 'to shake hands with your feet.'

I've been going to Mr Suddaby for years. I think it's an investment, particularly if you're like me and go in for slim-fitting court shoes (squeeze, squeeze). Mr Suddaby reads me the riot act, of course, but as he says, 'It's a free country, Miss Fozzard. If you want to open the door to a lifetime of hard skin, I can't stop you.' What view this Mr Dunderdale will take remains to be seen.

When I get back Mrs Beevers has her hat and coat on, can't wait to get off. Says Bernard has been propped up in a chair staring at the TV all evening. She helps me get him upstairs and then I sit by the bed and, as per the recovery programme, give him a run-down on my day.

Mr Clarkson-Hall down at the Unit says that when somebody has had a cerebral accident, 'In lay terms, a stroke, Miss Fozzard, we must take care not to treat them like a child. If your brother is going to recover his faculties, dear lady, the more language one can throw at him the better.'

I was just recounting my conversation with Mr Suddaby and how they're decamping to Scarborough when Bernard suddenly throws back his head and yawns.

I rang Mr Clarkson-Hall this morning. He says that's progress.

I do miss work.

I'M JUST GETTING MY THINGS on to go up to Mr Dunderdale's this evening, when Bernard has a little accident and manages to broadcast the entire contents of his bladder all the way down the stairs. Mrs Beevers is taking her time coming and it's only when I've got him all cleaned up and sitting on the throne that the doorbell eventually goes. Except even then it's not her, just a couple from church about Rwanda. I said, 'Never mind Rwanda, can we deal with the matter in hand and get a middle-aged gentleman off the lavatory?' So we get him downstairs and manoeuvre him onto his chosen chair five inches from the TV screen.

After they've gone I said, 'You can work the remote; it's about time you remembered how to wipe your own bottom.' Not a flicker. Of course, that's where they have you with a stroke: you never know what goes in and what doesn't.

When Mrs Beevers eventually does roll up she's half

an hour late which means I've missed the ten past and have to run all the way up Dyneley Road so by the time I'm ringing Mr Dunderdale's doorbell I'm all flustered and very conscious that my feet may be perspiring. He said, 'Well if that is what is troubling you, Miss Fozzard, I can straightaway put paid to the problem because I always kick off the proceedings by applying a mild astringent.'

Refined-looking feller, seventy-odd but with a lovely head of hair, one of the double-fronted houses that look over the cricket field. Rests my foot on a large silk handkerchief which I thought was a civilised touch; Mr Suddaby just used to use yesterday's *Evening Post*.

He said, 'Well, Miss Fozzard, I take one look at these and I say to myself here is someone who is on her feet a good deal. Am I right?' I said, 'You are. I'm in charge of the soft furnishing department at Matthias Robinson's, or was until my brother was taken ill. Anything you want in cretonne you know where to come.' He said, 'I might hold you to that but meanwhile could I compliment you on your choice of shoe.' I said, 'Well, as a rule I steer clear of suede because as a shoe it's a bit high maintenance, but sometimes I think the effort with the texturiser pays dividends.' He said, 'I can see we share a philosophy. If I may, I'll just begin by clipping your toenails.'

He said, 'Of course as soon as you walked in I picked you out as a professional woman.' I said, 'How?' He said, 'By your discreet choice of accessories.' I said, 'Well I favour a conservative approach to fashion, peppy but classic if you know what I mean.' He said, 'I do. There's been a verruca here, but it's extinct. Do you know why I chose the profession of chiropody?' I said, 'No.' He said, 'It's so that I could kneel at the feet of thousands of women and my wife would never turn a hair.' I said, 'Oh. Is there a Mrs Dunderdale?' He said, 'There was. She passed over.'

When he'd finished he rubbed in some mentholated oil (Moroccan apparently) and said I'd just feel a mild tingling effect which wasn't unpleasant and said my feet were in tip-top condition, the only possible cloud on the horizon a pre-fungal condition between two of my toes that he wanted to keep a watchful eye on.

Had on a lovely cardigan. I said, 'I hope you'll excuse me asking but is that cardigan cashmere?' He said, 'Well spotted, Miss Fozzard. This may be the first time you've seen it but it won't be the last, could I offer you a glass of sweet sherry?'

Churchwarden at St Wilfred's apparently, past president of the Inner Wheel and nicely off by the looks of it, a pillar of the community. When he's at the door he says, 'Next time, if you're very good, I shall initiate you into the mysteries of the metatarsal arch.'

I thought about it on the bus and when I gave Mrs Beevers her money I told her that with my wanting to get back to work she'd no need to come again as I was going to advertise for someone permanent. Bernard's got a bit put by and if this isn't a rainy day I don't know what is.

He was watching TV so I switched it off and took him through my evening as Mr Clarkson-Hall said I should. He looked a bit snotty but I said 'Bernard, nobody ever learned to talk again by watching the snooker.' Told him about Mr Dunderdale and the pre-fungal condition between my toes, his cashmere cardigan and whatnot.

As Mr Clarkson-Hall says, 'Miss Fozzard, it doesn't matter what you say so long as it's language: language is balls coming at you from every angle.' And it's working. I'd got him into bed and was just closing the door when I heard him say his first word. I think it was 'Cow'.

When I rang Mr Clarkson-Hall to tell him he said, 'Why cow?' I said, 'Probably an advert on TV.'

Still he agreed: it's a breakthrough.

IT WAS JUST that bit warmer today so I thought if I went along in my mustard Dannimac I could team it with my ancient peep-toe sandals that haven't had an airing since last summer when I had a little run over to Whitby with Joy Poyser.

Well, Mr Dunderdale couldn't get over them. Said he'd not seen a pair like them in fifteen years and that in the support they gave to the instep plus the unimpeded circulation of air via the toe no more sensible shoe had ever been devised. Made me parade up and down the room in them and would have taken a photograph only he couldn't put his hands on his Polaroid. Anyway I'm taking them along so that we can do it next time.

Wants me to go fortnightly until my *tinea pedis* yields to treatment but he's going to do it for the same fee and now that I'm back at work and we've got Miss Molloy coming in to see to Bernard there's no problem.

She said, 'Call me Mallory.' I said, 'Mallory? What sort of name is that? I wouldn't be able to put a sex to it.' She says, 'Well, I'm Australian.' Strong girl, very capable. And a qualified physiotherapist with a diploma in caring. It's Australian caring but I suppose it'll be the same as ours only minus the bugbear of hypothermia.

Ideally I would have preferred someone older, or someone less young anyway only we weren't exactly inundated with applicants which surprised me because I'd have thought it would have been a nice little side-line for a pensioner, though they'd have to be able-bodied. She chucks Bernard about as if he's two ha-porth of copper. Hails from Hobart, Tasmania, originally; I suppose England offers more scope for caring than the bush. And she and Bernard seem to hit it off, says she likes his sense of humour. I said to Joy Poyser, 'News to me. I didn't know he had one.'

Mind you, it's bearing fruit as movement's certainly coming back, he can hop up and down stairs now, more or less under his own steam. Speech too, because of course with him having company all day he gets the practice.

I was telling the whole saga of the stroke to Mr Dunderdale as he was tackling a patch of hard skin. He said, 'What did Bernard do, Miss Fozzard?' I said, 'Not to put too fine a point on it, Mr Dunderdale, he was a murderer. He said, 'Oh. That's unusual.' I said, 'Well, he was a tobacconist which comes to the same thing. Sweets and tobacco, a little kiosk in Headingley.' He said, 'Yes, well sweets and tobacco . . . it's a lethal combination.' I said, 'He smoked, he was overweight and he certainly liked a drink. Worry is another cause, I know, but as I said to Mr Clarkson-Hall that is something he never did. But now, of course he's paying for it. Only what seems unfair is that I'm paying for it too.'

Mr Dunderdale looked up and he said, 'Yes' (and he had my foot in his hand). He said, 'Yes. If there had been thirteen disciples instead of twelve, the other one would have been you Miss Fozzard.'

Green silk handkerchief this time. Last week it was red.

The words are beginning to come back, though, no doubt about it and when he can't manage a word I get him to do what Mr Clarkson-Hall suggested, namely describe what he means and skirt a path round it. Miss Molloy makes him do it as well and she says one way and another they get along. Bathes him every day, rubs him with baby oil, says that where bedsores are concerned prevention is better than cure.

I still go in on a night and give him all my news.

Mr Dunderdale had been saying that it was a pity evolution had taken the turn that it did because if it hadn't we might have found ourselves making as much use of our feet as we do our hands, which in the present economic climate might have been just what's needed to tip the balance. Miss Molloy said, 'That's interesting,' only Bernard just groans.

Personally I'm surprised she can put up with him but she says that by Australian standards he's a gentleman.

I hear them laughing.

SOFT FURNISHINGS, we're always a bit slack first thing so I'll generally do a little wander over into Floor Coverings and have a word with Estelle Metcalf. I wish it was Housewares we were next to as that would make it Joy Poyser because Estelle's all right but she's a bit on the young side, big glasses, boy friend's one of these who dress up as cavaliers at the weekend.

I said to her this morning, 'Shiatsu.' She said, 'Come again?' I said, 'Shiatsu, what is it?' She said, 'Is it a tropical fish?' I said, 'No.' She said, 'Is it a mushroom?' I said, 'No.' She said, 'Is it Mr Dunderdale?' I said, 'Why should it be Mr Dunderdale?' She said, 'Because most things are with you these days.' I said, 'I shall ignore that, Estelle. Suffice it to say it's a form of massage involving various pressure points on the body that was invented by the Japanese.' She said, 'That's all very well but it didn't stop them doing Pearl Harbour, did it?' Neville's besieging York on Sunday, trying out his new breastplate. Estelle's going along as an imploring housewife who comes out under a flag of truce.

Just then a customer comes in wanting some seersucker slipovers so we had to cut it short. I don't talk about Mr Dunderdale. And if I do she talks about Oliver Cromwell.

I go weekly now, though Mr Dunderdale won't charge me any more. I was sat on the sofa afterwards while he put away his instruments and he said, 'Good news, Miss Fozzard. We seem to have cracked the *tinea pedis*, not a trace of it left. I think that calls for a sherry refill. Are you in a hurry to get off?' I said, 'No. Why?' He said, 'Well, we still have a little time in hand and I wonder if I might prevail upon you to try on a pair of bootees?' I said, 'Bootees?'

He said, 'Well, I'm using the term loosely. They're technically what we would call a fur-lined Gibson bruised look but bootees is a convenient shorthand. The shade is Bengal bronze.' I said, 'Well, they're a lovely shoe.' He said, 'Yes. Cosy, ankle-hugging they make a beautiful ending to the leg. They're a present, of course.' I said, 'Oh, Mr Dunderdale, I couldn't.' He said, 'Miss Fozzard, please. My contacts in the world of footwear procure me a considerable discount. Besides there is a little something you can do for me in return.' I said, 'Oh?' He said, 'My years in bending over ladies' feet have resulted in an intermittently painful condition of the lower back which, if you are amenable you have it in your power to alleviate.' I said, 'I do, Mr Dunderdale?' He said, 'You do, Miss Fozzard. I'm going to put one cushion on the hearthrug here for my head and the other here for my abdomen and now I'm going to lie down and what I want you to do is to step on my lower back.' I said, 'Should I take the bootees off?' He said, 'No, no. Keep the bootees on, their texture makes them ideal for the purpose. That's it. Steady yourself by holding onto the edge of the mantelpiece if you want.'

Then he said something I couldn't hear because his face was pressed into the carpet. 'What was that, Mr Dunderdale?' 'I said, "Excellent," Miss Fozzard. You may move about a little if you would care to.' I said, 'I'm anxious not to hurt you, Mr Dunderdale.' He said,

'Have no fears on that score, Miss Fozzard. Trample away.' I said, 'I feel like one of those French peasants treading the grapes.' He said, 'Yes. Yes, yes.' I said, 'Do you feel the benefit?' He said, 'Yes, yes, I do. Thank you. If you don't mind, Miss Fozzard I'll just lie here for a little while. Perhaps you could see yourself out.'

So I just left him on the hearthrug.

When I got back Bernard is sitting on the sofa with Miss Molloy, both of them looking a bit red in the face. 'We were just laughing,' Miss Molloy says, 'because Bernard couldn't think of a word.' 'Well,' I said, 'he must learn to skirt round it.' 'Oh, he did that all right,' she said. 'You're an expert at that, aren't you Bernard?' And they both burst out laughing.

Mr Clarkson-Hall's very pleased with him. Says he's never known a recovery so quick. Says he didn't have the privilege of knowing Bernard before but he imagines he's now quite like his old self. I said, 'Yes. He is.'

After Miss Molloy had gone he comes in here while I'm having my hot drink and says he's thinking of opening the kiosk again and that Mallory is going to help him. I said, 'Does Miss Molloy have any experience of sweets and tobacco?' He said, 'No, but she's a fun-loving girl with a welcoming whatever it's called and that's half the battle.'

Note from Mr Dunderdale this morning saying his back is much better and that he was looking forward to seeing me next week.

Estelle suffers in the back department, the legacy from once having had to wield a spare pike at the Battle of Naseby. So I was telling her all about me helping Mr Dunderdale with his, only she wasn't grateful. Just giggles and says, 'Ooh, still waters!'

Floor coverings, they ought to have somebody more mature. She really belongs in Cosmetics.

I DON'T KNOW what's got into people at work. I come in this morning and the commissionaire with the moustache who's on the staff door says, 'Have a good day, my duck.' I said, 'You may only have one arm, Mr Capstick, but that doesn't entitle you to pat me on the bottom.' Next thing is I'm invoicing some loose covers in Despatch when one of the work experience youths who can't be more than sixteen gives me a silly wink.

I said to Estelle, 'My Viyella two-piece doesn't normally have this effect.' She said, 'Well they're just wanting to be friendly.' I said, 'Friendly? Estelle, I may not be a feminist (though I did spearhead the provision of pot-pourri in the ladies toilets) but people are not going to pat my bottom with impunity.' Estelle says, 'No. The boot's on the other foot,' and starts giggling. I said to Joy Poyser, 'How ever she manages to interest anyone in serious vinyl flooring I do not understand.'

House dark when I got in. I imagine they're in the sitting room, the pair of them only I call out and there's no sound. So I get my tea and read the *Evening Post*, nice to have the place to myself for a change.

Then I go into the sitting room and there's Bernard sitting there in the dark. I put the light on and he's got the atlas open. I said, 'What are you doing in the dark?' He said, 'Looking up the Maldive Islands.' 'Why,' I said, 'you're not going on holiday?' He said, 'No, I'm not. How can I go on bloody holiday? What with?' And he shoves a bank statement at me.

I've a feeling he's been crying and I'm not sure where to put myself so I go put the kettle on while I look at his statement. There's practically nothing in it, money taken out nearly every day. I said, 'What's this?' He said, 'It's that tart from Hobart.' I said, 'Miss Molloy? But she's a qualified physiotherapist.' He said, 'Yes and she's something else . . . she's a—what do you call it—female dog.'

I said, 'Did you sign these cheques?' He said, 'Of course I signed them.' I said, 'What were you doing, practising writing?' He said, 'No.' I said, 'Where is she?' He said, 'The Maldive Islands, where I was going to be.' I said, 'Well we must contact the police. It's fraud is this.' He said, 'No it isn't.' I said, 'What did you think these cheques were for?' He said, 'I knew what they were for. For services rendered. And I don't mean lifting me on and off the what's it called. It's stuff she did for me.' I said, 'What stuff?' He said, 'You know.'

I said, 'Remember what Mr Clarkson-Hall says, Bernard. Trace a path round the word.' He said, 'I don't have to trace a path round the bloody word. I know the word. It's you that doesn't. You don't know bloody nothing.' I said, 'Well one thing is plain. Despite your cerebral accident your capacity for foul language remains unimpaired.' He said, 'You're right. It bloody does.'

I made him some tea. I said, 'She's made a fool of you.' Bernard said, 'You can speak.' I said. 'You mean talk. I know I can speak. The expression is, you can talk. Anyway why?' He said, 'Monkeying about with your foot feller.' I said, 'Mr Dunderdale? What's he got to do with it?' He said, 'Little games and whatnot. He's obviously a . . . a . . . .' I said, 'A what?' He said, 'A . . . thing.' I said, 'Skirt a path round the word, Bernard.

A what?' He said, 'Skirt it yourself you stupid . . . four legs, two horns, where you get milk.' I said, 'Cow. You normally remember that.'

I was telling Joy Poyser about it and she said, 'Well, why did you tell him about the chiropodist?' I said, 'Mr Clarkson-Hall said that I should talk to him, it's part of the therapy.' She said, 'It's not part of the therapy for Estelle Metcalf, is it? You told her. She's not had a stroke.' Apparently she's spread it all over the store.

Anyway I came upstairs, left him crying over the atlas, when suddenly I hear a crash. I said, 'Bernard? Bernard?'

'BERNARD!'

ESTELLE VENTURED into Soft Furnishings yesterday, first time for a week. Testing the water, I suppose. Said Neville was taking part in the battle of Marston Moor on Sunday. She's going along as a camp follower but they're short of one or two dishevelled Roundhead matrons and was I interested? I said, 'It's kind of you to offer, Estelle, but I think from now I'd be well advised to keep a low profile.'

People don't like to think you have a proper life,

that's what I've decided. Or any more of a life than they know about. Then when they find out they think it's shocking. Else funny. I never thought I had a life. It was always Bernard who had the life.

He's worse this time than the last. Eyes used to follow you then. Not now. Log. Same rigmarole, though. Talk to him. Treat him like a person. Not that he ever treated me like a person. Meanwhile Madam is laid out on the beach in the Maldives. He was on the rug when I found him. Two inches the other way and he'd have hit his head on the fender. Lucky escape.

I'd written to Mr Dunderdale, cancelling any further appointments. I didn't say why, just that with Bernard being poorly again it wasn't practical anyway. Which it wasn't.

So it was back to normal, sitting with Bernard, doing a few little jobs. I'd forgotten how long an evening could be.

Anyway, I was coming away from work one night and a big browny-coloured car draws up beside me, the window comes down and blow me if it isn't Mr Dunderdale.

He said, 'Good evening, Miss Fozzard. Could I tempt you up to Lawnswood? I'd like a little chat.' I said, 'Could we not talk here?' He said, 'Not in the way I'd like. I'm on a double yellow line.' So I get in and he runs me up there and whatever else you can say about him he's a very accomplished driver.

Anyway he sits me down in his study and gives me a glass of sherry and says why did I not want to come and see him any more. Well, I didn't know what to say. I said, 'It isn't as if I don't look forward to my appointments.' He said, 'Well, dear lady, I look forward to them too.' I said, 'But now that I have to get help in for Bernard again I can't afford to pay you.'

He said, 'Well, may I make a suggestion? Why don't we reverse the arrangement?' I said, 'Come again.' He said, 'Do it vice versa. I pay you.' I said, 'Well, it's very unusual.' He said, 'You're a very unusual woman.' I said, 'I am? Why?' He said, 'Because you're a free spirit, Miss Fozzard. You make your own rules.' I said, 'Well, I like to think so.' He said, 'I'm the same. We're two of a kind, you and I, Miss Fozzard. Mavericks. Have you ever had any champagne?' I said, 'No, but I've seen it at the conclusion of motor races.' He said, 'Allow me. To the future?'

It's all very decorous. Quite often he'll make us a hot drink and we'll just sit and turn over the pages of one of his many books on the subject, or converse on matters related. I remarked the other day how I'd read that Imelda Marcos had a lot of shoes. He said, 'She did . . . and she suffered for it at the bar of world opinion, in my view, Miss Fozzard, unjustly.'

Little envelope on the hall table as I go out, never mentioned, and if there's been anything beyond the call of duty there'll be that little bit extra. Buys me no end of shoes, footwear generally. I keep thinking where's it all going to end but we'll walk that plank when we come to it.

I've never had the knack of making things happen. I thought things happened or they didn't. Which is to say they didn't. Only now they have . . . sort of.

Bernard gets an attendance allowance now and what with that and the envelopes from Mr Dunderdale I can stay on at work and still have someone in to look after him. Man this time. Mr Albright. Pensioner, so he's glad of a job. Classy little feller, keen on railways and reckons to be instigating Bernard into the mysteries of chess. Though Mr Albright has to play both sides of course.

At one point I said to Mr Dunderdale, 'People might think this rather peculiar particularly in Lawnswood.' He said, 'Well, people would be wrong. We are just enthusiasts, Miss Fozzard, you and I and there's not enough enthusiasm in the world these days. Now if those Wellingtons are comfy I just want you in your own time and as slowly as you like very gently to mark time on my bottom.'

Occasionally he'll have some music on. I said once, 'I suppose that makes this the same as aerobics.' He said, 'If you like.'

It's droll but the only casualty in all this is my feet, because nowadays the actual chiropody gets pushed to one side a bit. If I want an MOT I really have to nail him down.

We're still Mr Dunderdale and Miss Fozzard and I've not said anything to anybody at work. Learned my lesson there.

Anyway, people keep saying how well I look.

I SUPPOSE THERE'S A WORD for what I'm doing but . . . I skirt round it.

Father! Father!

Burning Bright

On the many occasions Midgley had killed his father, death had always come easily. He died promptly, painlessly and without a struggle. Looking back, Midgley could see that even in these imagined deaths he had failed his father. It was not like him to die like that. Nor did he.

The timing was good, Midgley acknowledged that. Only his father would have managed to stage his farewell in the middle of a 'Meet The Parents' week. It was not a function Midgley enjoyed. Each year he was dismayed how young the parents had grown, the youth of fathers in particular. Most sported at least one tattoo, with ears and noses now routinely studded. Midgley saw where so many of his pupils got it from. One father wore a swastika necklace, of the sort Midgley had wondered if he felt justified in confiscating from a boy. And a mother he had talked to had had green hair. 'Not just green,' muttered Miss Tunstall, 'bright green. And then you wonder the girls get pregnant.'

That was the real point of these get-togethers. The teachers were appalled by the parents but found their shortcomings reassuring. With parents like these, they reasoned, who could blame the schools? The parents, recalling their own teachers as figures of dignity and authority, found the staff sloppy. Awe never entered into it, apparently. 'Too human by half' was their verdict. So both Nature and Nurture came away, if not satisfied, at any rate absolved. 'Do you wonder?' said the teachers, looking at the parents. 'They get it at school,' said the parents.

'Coretta's bin havin' these massive monthlies. Believe me, Mr Midgley, I en never seen menstruatin' like it.' Mrs Azakwale was explaining her daughter's poor showing in Use of English. 'She bin wadin' about in blood to her ankles, Mr Midgley. I en never out of the launderette.' Behind Mrs Azakwale, Mr Horsfall listened openly and with unconcealed scepticism, shaking his head slowly as Midgley caught his eye. Behind Mr Horsfall, Mr Patel beamed with embarrassment as the large black woman said these terrible things so loudly. And beyond Mr Patel, Midgley saw the chairs were empty.

Mrs Azakwale took Coretta's bloodstained track-record over to the queue marked Computer Sciences, leaving Midgley faced with Mr Horsfall and Martin.

Mr Horsfall did not dye his hair nor wear an earring. His hair was now fashionably short but only because he had never got round to wearing it fashionably long. Nor had his son Martin ever ventured under the drier; his ears, too, were intact. Mr Horsfall was a detective sergeant.

'I teach Martin English, Mr Horsfall,' said Midgley, wishing he had not written 'Hopeless' on Martin's report, a document now gripped by Mr Horsfall in his terrible policeman's hand.

'Martin? Is that what you call him?'

'But that's his name.' Midgley had a moment of wild anxiety that it wasn't, that the father would accuse him of not even knowing the name of his son.

'His name's Horsfall. Martin is what we call him, his mother and me. For your purposes I should have thought his name was Horsfall. Are you married?'

'Yes.'

Horsfall was not impressed. He had spent long vigils in public toilets as a young constable. Many of the patrons had turned out to be married and some of them teachers. Marriage involved no medical examination, no questionnaire to speak of. Marriage for these people was just the bush they hid behind.

'What does my son call you?'

'He calls me Mr Midgley.'

'Doesn't he call you sir?'

'On occasion.'

'Schools . . .' Horsfall sniffed.

His son ought to have been small, nervous and bright, Midgley the understanding schoolteacher taking his part against his big, overbearing parent. He would have put books into his hands, watched him flower so that in time to come the boy would look back and think 'Had it not been for him . . .' Such myths sustained Midgley when he woke in the small hours of the morning and drowsed during the middle period of the afternoon. But they were myths. Martin was large and dull. He was not unhappy. He would not flower. He was not even embarrassed. He was probably on his father's side, thought Midgley, as he sat there looking at his large inherited hands, and occasionally picked at one of a scattering of violet-painted warts.

'What worries me,' said Horsfall, 'is that he can scarcely put two words together.'

This was particularly hurtful to a man who, in his

professional capacity, specialised in converting the faltering confessions of semi-illiterates into his plain policeman's prose. He could do it. At four o'clock in the morning after a day spent combing copses and dragging ponds, never mind house-to-house enquiries, he could do it. Why not his son?

'You show me up, Martin, having to come along here. I don't grudge coming along here. But what I would like to have come along here as is a proud father. To be told of your achievements. Be shown your name in gilt letters on the honours board. Martin Horsfall. But no. What is it? It's Geography: Poor. History: Poor. English: Hopeless. PE: Only fair. Why Martin?'

'Why Mr Midgley? And why hopeless? Geography: Poor. History: Poor. English: Hopeless. Is he hopeless or are you?'

'He doesn't try.'

'Do you challenge him? We challenge him at home. His mother and I challenge him. Does he get challenged at school? I don't see it.' Horsfall looked round but caught the eye of Mr Patel, who was smiling in anticipation of his interview. Mr Patel's son was clever. Blacks, Indians. That was why. Challenge. How could there be any challenge?

'I never had chances like he had. And I dare say you didn't. We never had chances like that, Martin.'

At the 'we' Midgley flinched, suddenly finding himself handcuffed to Horsfall in the same personal pronoun.

'A school like this. Modern buildings. Light. Air. Sporting facilities tip-top. Volleyball. If somebody had come up to me when I was your age and said "There are facilities for volleyball", I would have gone down on my knees. What do you say?'

The question Horsfall was asking his son had no obvious answer. Indeed, it was not really a question at all. 'Justify your life'; that was what this dull and dirty youth was being asked to do. Not seeing that justification was necessary, the son was silent and the father waited.

And it was in the middle of this silence that Miss Tunstall came up to say the hospital had telephoned. Except that, sensing this was not simply a silence but an essential part of what was being said, she did not immediately interrupt but made little wavings with her hand behind Mr Horsfall's head, who—a policeman and ever on the watch for mockery—turned round. So it was to him that Miss Tunstall gave the bad news (a man in any case used to transactions with ambulances, hospitals and all the regimes of crisis).

'The hospital's just rung. Mr Midgley's father's been taken ill.' And only then, having delivered her message did she look at Midgley, who thus heard his father was dying at second-hand and then only as a kind of apology.

'They're ringing the ward,' said Midgley. 'It's a fall, apparently.' One ear was in Miss Tunstall's office, the other fifty miles away in some nowhere behind a switchboard.

'You want to pray it's not his hip,' said Miss Tunstall. 'That's generally the weak spot.' She had a mother of her own. 'The pelvis heals in no time, surprisingly.' She did not sound surprised. Her mother had broken her pelvis and she had thought it was the beginning of the end. 'No. It's when it's the hip it's complicated.'

'Switchboard's on the blink,' said a voice.

'Join the club,' said another. 'I've been on the blink all day.'

'It's the dreaded lurgi,' said the first voice.

'Hello,' said Midgley. But there was silence.

'She took a nasty tumble in Safeway's last week,' went on Miss Tunstall. 'They do when they get older.

It's what you must expect.' She expected it all the time. 'Their bones get brittle.'

She cracked her fingers and adjusted the spacing.

'Maintenance,' said a new voice.

'I've been wrongly connected,' said Midgley.

'It's these ancillary workers,' said Miss Tunstall. 'Holding the country to ransom. Other people's suffering is their bread and butter.' She was wanting to get on with a notice about some boys acting the goat in the swimming baths but felt she ought to wait until Midgley had heard one way or the other. Her mother was 82. The last twenty years had not been easy and had she known what was in store she thought now she would probably have stabbed her mother to death the second she turned 60. These days it would only have meant a suspended sentence or if the worst came to the worst open prison. Miss Tunstall had once been round such an institution with the school and found it not uncongenial. A picnic in fact.

'Records are on the warpath again,' said a voice in Midgley's ear.

'It never rains,' said another.

'Should I be sterilisin' this?' said a black voice.

'Search me, dear,' said an emancipated one.

'Hello,' said Midgley. 'HELLO.'

Softly Miss Tunstall began to type.

Midgley thought of his father lying in bed, dying but not wanting to be any trouble.

'No joy?' said Miss Tunstall, uncertain whether it would be better to underline 'the likelihood of a serious accident'. 'And then they wonder why people are stampeding to BUPA.'

Midgley decided he had been forgotten then a crisp voice suddenly said 'Sister Tudor'.

'I'm calling about a patient, a Mr Midgley.'

Noiselessly Miss Tunstall added an exclamation mark to 'This hooliganism must now STOP!' and waited, her hands spread over the keys.

'What is the patient's name?'

'Midgley,' said Midgley. 'He came in this morning.'

'When was he admitted?'

'This morning.'

'Midgley.' There was a pause. 'We have no Midgley. No Midgley has been admitted here. Are you sure you have the right ward?'

'He was admitted this morning. I was told he was seriously ill.'

'Oh yes.' Her tone changed. 'Midgley. What is your name?'

'Midgley.'

'Are you next of kin?'

'My father is dead,' he thought. 'Only the dead have next of kin.'

'I'm his son.'

Miss Tunstall folded her hands in her lap.

'He's not at all well.' The tone was reproachful rather than sympathetic. 'We think he's had a stroke. He's been lying on the floor. He ought to have been in hospital sooner. There's now the question of pneumonia. It's touch and go.'

'It's touch and go,' said Midgley, putting the phone down.

'How old is he?' said Miss Tunstall, noticing she had typed 'tooling' for 'fooling'.

'He's 74.'

Her mother was 82. She ripped out the paper and wound in another sheet. Life was unfair.

The door opened.

'Been on the phone again Midgley?' said the headmaster. 'I'm the one who has to go cap in hand to the Finance Committee.'

'Mr Midgley's father's ill,' said Miss Tunstall, once again the apologetic herald. 'Apparently it's touch and go.'

And she started typing like the wind.

'Of course you can go. Of course you must go. One's father. There can be no question. A filial obligation.' Midgley was in the headmaster's study. 'It's awkward, of course. But then it always is.' It was death. It was a reshuffling of the timetable.

Midgley's thoughts were with his father in Intensive Care.

'Was he getting on in years?'

No effort was being spared to keep him alive and in the present and yet grammatically he kept slipping into the past.

'He's 74.'

'Seventy-four. Once upon a time I thought that was old. You won't be gone long? What, three, four days?' In his mind the headmaster roughed out a timetable whereby Midgley senior could decently die, be buried and Midgley junior be back in harness. Radical surgery on the timetable might still be avoided.

'Let me see. It's English, Integrated Humanities and Creative Arts, nothing else, is there?'

'Environmental Studies.'

The headmaster groaned. 'That's the awkward one. Pilbeam's off on another course. That's the trouble with the environment, it involves going on courses. I'll be glad when the environment is confined to the textbooks.'

'Ah well,' said the headmaster. 'It can't be helped.' He had never understood the fuss people made about their parents. 'Both of mine were despatched years ago. A flying bomb.' He made it sound like a victory for common sense.

'He must have fallen and not been able to get up,' said Midgley. 'He was lying there two days.'

'An all too familiar scenario these days,' said the headmaster. 'Isolated within the community. Alone in the crowd. You must not feel guilty.'

'I generally go over at weekends,' said Midgley.

'It will give Tomlinson an opportunity to do some of his weird and wonderful permutations with the timetable. Though I fear this one will tax even Tomlinson's talents.'

The headmaster opened the door.

'One must hope it is not as grave as it appears. One must hope he turns the corner. Corners seem to have gone out of medicine nowadays. In the old days the sick were always turning them. Illness is now much more of a straight road. Why is that?'

It was not a question he wanted answering.

FATHER! FATHER! BURNING BRIGHT

'Antibiotics?' said Midgley, lingering.

'Sometimes one has the impression modern medicine encourages patients to loiter.' It was Midgley who was taking his time.

'Mistakenly, one feels. God speed.'

Miss Tunstall had finished the notice about acting the goat in the swimming baths and the headmaster now glanced through it, taking out his pen. She made a start on another notice about the bringing of pupils' cars to school, one of the head's 'privilege not a right' notices. Midgley still hesitated.

'I'm not sure if we've couched this in strong enough terms, Daphne.'

'It's as you dictated it.'

'I have no doubt. But I feel more strongly about it now. Nothing else is there, Midgley?'

Midgley shook his head and went out.

'A boy slips. Is pushed and we are talking about concussion. A broken neck. A fatality, Daphne. I intend to nail the culprits. I want them to know they will be crucified.'

'Shall I put that?'

The headmaster looked at her sharply and wondered if Miss Tunstall was through the menopause.

'We must find a paraphrase. But first the problems

caused by this business of Midgley père. Ask Tomlinson to step over will you, Daphne. Tell him to bring his coloured pencils. And a rubber.'

'Tomato or my jam?'

'Tomato.'

The hospital was fifty miles away. His wife was making him sandwiches. He sat in his raincoat at the kitchen table, watching her apply a faint smear of Flora to the wholemeal bread.

'I wanted to go over this last weekend,' said Midgley. 'I would have gone over if your Margaret hadn't suddenly descended.'

'You knew they were coming. They'd been coming for weeks. It's one of the few things Mother's got to look forward to.' Mrs Midgley's mother was stood staring out of the window. 'Don't blame our Margaret.'

'I just never expected it,' said Midgley.

If you expected something it didn't happen.

'I expected it,' said his wife, putting on a shiny plastic apron emblazoned with a portrait of Sylvia Plath.

'I expected it. Last time I went over he came to the door to wave me off. He's never done that before. Bless him.' She slipped on a pair of padded Union Jack mittens and sinking to her knees before the oven gave the Shift a trial blast. 'I think people know.'

'He does come to the door,' said Midgley. 'He always comes to the door.' And it was true he did, but only, Midgley felt, to show that the visit had been so short it needed extending. Though once, catching sight of him in the rear-view mirror, waving, Midgley had cried.

'He was trying to tell me something,' said his wife. 'I know a farewell when I see one.' A fine spray misted the oven's pale grey walls. 'Shouldn't you be going?'

'Is it Saturday today?' said her mother.

Ten minutes later Midgley was sitting on the stairs and his wife had started hoovering.

'I'm not going to let him down. I want to be there when he goes,' shouted Midgley.

The vacuum was switched off.

'What?'

'He loved me.'

'I can't think why,' said Midgley's wife. 'It's not as if you take after him,' and she switched on again, 'not one little bit.'

'Joyce,' her mother called, 'when is that chiropodist coming?'

Midgley looked at his watch. It was three o'clock. At ten past Mrs Midgley took to dusting. It was always assumed the housework put her in a bad temper. The truth was if she was in a bad temper she did the house-work. So it came to the same thing.

'He had strength,' she said, dusting a group of lem-onade bottles of various ages. 'Our Colin is going to be strong. He loved Colin.'

'Does he know?' asked Midgley.

'Yes. Only it hasn't hit him yet.'

Hoarse shouting and a rhythmic drumming on the floor indicated that his son was seeking solace in music.

'When it does hit him,' said his mother, picking at a spot of rust on a recently acquired Oxo tin, 'he is going to be genuinely heartbroken. There's always a gap. It was on *Woman's Hour*. Poor old Frank.'

'I've never understood,' said Midgley, 'why you call him Frank. He's my father.'

She looked at the 1953 Coronation mug, wonder-ing if it was altogether too recent an artefact to have on display.

'He has a name. Frank is his name.'

It was not only the date, the Coronation mug was about the only object in the house Midgley had con-tributed to the decor, having been issued with it in 1953 when he was at primary school.

'I call him Dad,' said Midgley.

'He's not Dad, is he? Not my dad, I call him Frank because that's the name of a person. To me he is a person. That's why we get on.'

She was about to hide the mug behind a cast-iron money-box in the shape of a grinning black man then thought better of it. They had too many things. And there would be more coming from his dad. She cheered up slightly.

Her husband kissed her and opened the back door.

'It isn't though,' he said.

'It isn't what?'

'Why you get on. Treating him like a person.'

Seeing her stood there in her silly apron he felt sorry for her, and wished he had kept quiet.

'You get on,' he said (and because he was sorry for her tried to make it sound as if she was justified), 'you get on because you both despise me.'

'Listen.' She brought him away from the door and closed it. Mrs Barnes next door, who had once described their marriage as uninhibited, was putting out a few opportune clothes. 'Your father is 74. He is dying. Considering the time you've been hanging about here he is possibly already dead yet you resent the fact that he and I were friends. I seem to have married someone very low down in the evolutionary chain. You might want one or two tissues.' And she darted at him and thrust them into his pocket.

Midgley opened the door again.

'It's just that when you and he were together I didn't exist.'

'I am married,' she shouted, 'to the cupboard under the sink.' A remark made more mysterious to Mrs Barnes by the sound of a passing ice-cream van playing the opening bars of the 'Blue Danube'.

'He is *dying*, Denis. Will you exist now? Will that satisfy you?' She was crying.

'I'll make it right, Joyce,' said Midgley. 'I'll be there when he goes. I'll hold his hand.'

He held hers, still in their Union Jack mittens. 'If I let him down now he'd stay with me the rest of my life. I did love him, Joyce.'

'I *want* him to stay with you the rest of your life. That's what I want. I think of his kindness. His unselfishness. His unflagging courtesy. The only incredible thing is that someone so truly saintly should have produced such a pill of a son.'

She took off Sylvia Plath and hung her behind the door. She had stopped crying.

'But I suppose that's your mother.'

'Shut up about my mother,' said Midgley.

His mother was a sore point. 'My mother is dead.'

'So is your father by now probably. Go!'

Midgley took her by the shoulders.

'Things will change then, you'll see. I'll change. I'll be a different person. I can . . . go. Live! Start!' He kissed her quickly and warmly and ran from the door down the little drive towards the van. His wife rushed to the door to catch him.

'Start?' she shouted. 'Start what? You're 39.'

'They had another do today,' Mrs Barnes told her husband that evening. 'It doesn't say much for a university education.'

COMING OFF THE Leeds and Bradford Ring Road Midgley stopped at a zebra to let an old man cross. The old man held up a warning hand, and slowly moved across, glowering at the car. Midgley revved his engine and the old man stopped, glared and went on with seemingly deliberate slowness. Someone behind hooted. Midgley did not wait for the old man to reach the kerb but drove off with a jerk. Glancing in his mirror Midgley saw the old man slip and nearly fall.

At the hospital the first person he saw was Aunty Kitty, his father's sister. She said nothing, kissing him wordlessly, her eyes closed to indicate her grief lay temporarily beyond speech. The scene played she took his arm (something he disliked) and they followed the signs to Intensive Care.

'I thought you'd have been here a bit since,' said his Aunty. 'I've been here since two o'clock. You'll notice a big change.' They were going down a long featureless corridor. 'He's not like my brother. He's not the Frank I knew.' Visitors clustered at the doors of-wards, waiting their turn to sit beside the beds of loved ones. Aunty Kitty favoured them with a brave smile. 'I don't dislike this colour scheme,' she said. 'I've always liked oatmeal. His doctor's black.'

Intensive Care had a waiting room to itself, presum-ably, Midgley thought, for the display of Intensive Grief, and there was a woman crying in the corner. 'Her hubby's on the critical list,' mouthed Aunty Kitty. 'Their eldest girl works for Johnson and Johnson. They'd just got back from Barbados. The nurse is white but she's not above eighteen.' The nurse came in. 'This is my nephew,' said Aunty Kitty. 'Mr Midg-ley's son. Your father's got a room to himself, love.'

'They all do,' said the nurse, 'at this stage.'

Midgley's father lay propped up against the pillows, staring straight ahead through the window at a blank yellow wall. His arms lay outside the coverlet, palms upward as if accepting his plight and awaiting some sort of deliverance. They had put him into some green hospital pyjamas, with half-length sleeves the function-alism of which seemed too modish to Midgley, who had only ever seen his father in bed in striped pyjamas, or sometimes his shirt. The garment was open and a monitor clung to his chest, and above the bed the tele-vision screen blipped steady and regular. Midgley watched it for a moment.

'Dad,' he said to himself.

'Dad. It's me, Denis.'

He put himself between the bed and the window so that if his father could see he would know he was there. He had read that stroke victims were never un-conscious, just held incommunicado. 'In the most sol-itary confinement,' the article had said, the writer himself a doctor and too much taken with metaphor.

'It's all right, Dad.'

He took a chair and sat halfway down the bed, put-ting his hand over his father's inert palm.

His father looked well in the face, which was ruddy and worn, the skin of his neck giving way sharply to the white of his body. The division between his known head and the unknown body had shocked Midgley

when he had first seen it as a child, when his Dad took
him swimming at the local baths. It was still the same.
He had never sat in the sun all his life.

'I'm sorry, Dad,' said Midgley.

'Are you next of kin?' It was another nurse.

'Son.'

'Not too long then.'

'Is the doctor around?'

'Why? What do you want to know? There's nothing wrong, is there? No complaints?'

'I want to know how he is.'

'He's very poorly. You can see.'

She looked down at her left breast and lifted a
watch.

'Doctor'll be round in about an hour. He's very
busy.'

'I wonder where he is,' said Aunty Kitty.

'She said he was busy.'

They were back in the waiting room.

Aunty Kitty looked at him with what he imagined
she imagined was a look of infinite sadness, mingled
with pity ('Sorrow and love flow mingling down'
came into his mind from the hymn). 'Not the doctor,
your dad, love. Behind that stare he's somewhere,

wandering. You know,' she said vaguely, 'in his mind. Where is he?'

She patted his hand.

'I don't suppose with having been to university you believe in an after-life. That's always the first casualty.'

For a while she read the small print on her pension book and Midgley thought about his childhood. Nurses came and went, leading their own lives and a man wiped plastic-covered mattresses in the corridor. Every time a nurse came near he made remarks like 'It's all right for some' or 'No rest for the wicked.' Once the matron glided silently by, majestic and serene on her electric trolley. 'They're a new departure,' said Aunty Kitty. 'I could do with one of those. I'll just pop and have another peep at your dad.'

'What does that look on his face mean?' she said when she came back. Midgley thought it meant he should have gone over to see him last Sunday. It meant that his dad had been right about him all along and now he was dying and whose fault was that? That was what it meant. 'This unit was opened by the Duchess of Kent,' said Aunty Kitty. 'They have a tip-top kidney department.'

The fascinations of medicine and royalty were equal

in Aunty Kitty's mind and whenever possible she found a connection between the two. Had she been told she was dying but from the same disease as a member of the Royal Family she would have died happy.

'There's some waiting done in hospitals,' she said presently. 'Ninety per cent of it's waiting. Would you call this room oatmeal or cream?'

A young man came through, crying.

'His wife was in an accident,' Aunty Kitty explained. 'One of those head-on crashes. The car was a write-off. Did you come in your van?'

Midgley nodded.

'You'll be one of these two-car families, then? Would you say she was black?' A Thai nurse looked in briefly and went out again. 'You don't see that many of them. She's happen a refugee.'

Midgley looked at his watch. It was an hour since he had spoken to the nurse. He went in and stood at the desk but there was no one about. He stood at the door of his father's room. He had not moved, his unseeing eyes fixed on a window-cleaner, who with professional discretion carefully avoided their gaze.

'I always thought I'd be the first to go,' said Aunty Kitty, looking at an advertisement in *Country Life*. 'Fancy. Two swimming pools. I could do without two swimming pools. When you get to my age you just want somewhere you can get round nicely with the hoover. They've never got to the bottom of my complaint. They lowered a microscope down my throat but there was nothing. I wouldn't live in Portugal if they paid me. Minstrels' gallery, I shouldn't know what to do with a minstrels' gallery if I had one. Mr Penry-Jones wanted to put me on this machine the Duke of Gloucester inaugurated. This body-scan thing. Only there was such a long waiting-list apparently.'

A nurse came through.

'She's the one I was telling you about. I asked her if your dad was in a coma or just unconscious. She didn't know. They're taking them too young these days.'

'Aunty,' said Midgley.

'It isn't as if she was black. Black you don't expect them to know.'

'What was my dad like?'

Aunty Kitty thought for a moment.

'He never had a wrong word for anybody. He'd do anybody a good turn. Shovel their snow. Fetch their coal in. He was that type. He was a saint. You take after your mother more.'

'I feel I lack his sterling qualities,' said Midgley some

time later. 'Grit. Patience. Virtues bred out of adver-
sity.'

'You wouldn't think they'd have curtains in a hospital, would you?' said Aunty Kitty. 'You wouldn't
think curtains would be hygienic. I'm not keen on
purple anyway.'

'Deprivation for instance,' said Midgley.

'What?'

'I was never deprived. That way he deprived me.
Do you understand?'

'I should have gone to secondary school,' she said.
'I left at thirteen, same as your dad.'

'I know I had it easier than he did,' said Midgley.
'But I was grateful. I didn't take it for granted.'

'You used to look bonny in your blazer.'

'It isn't particularly enjoyable, education.' Midgley
had his head in his hands. 'I had what he wanted. Why
should that be enjoyable?'

'Mark's got his bronze medal,' said Aunty Kitty.
'Did you not ought to be ringing round?'

'About the bronze medal?'

'About your dad.'

'I'll wait till I've seen the doctor.'

It was half-past six.

'They go on about these silicon chips, you'd think

they'd get all these complaints licked first, somebody's got their priorities wrong. Then he's always been a right keen smoker has Frank. Now he's paying the price.'

Midgley fell asleep.

'Robert Donat had bronchitis,' said Aunty Kitty.

'MR MIDGLEY.' The doctor shook his shoulder.

'Denis,' said Aunt Kitty, 'it's doctor.'

He was a pale young Pakistani, and for a moment Midgley thought he had fallen asleep in class and was being woken by a pupil.

'Mr Midgley?' He was grave and precise, 26 at the most.

'Your father has had a stroke.' He looked at his clip-board. 'How severe it is hard to tell. When he was brought in he was suffering from hypothermia.'

Aunt Kitty gave a faint cry. It was a scourge that had been much in the news.

'He must have fallen and been lying there, two days at least.'

'I generally go over at weekends,' said Midgley.

'Pneumonia has set in. His heart is not strong. All things considered,' he looked at the clipboard again, 'we do not think he will last the night.'

As he went away he tucked the clipboard under his arm and Midgley saw there was nothing on it.

'ONLY THREE PHONES and two of them duff. You wouldn't credit it,' said a fat man. 'Say you were on standby for a transplant. It'd be just the same.' He jingled his coins and a young man in glasses on the working phone put his head outside the helmet.

'I've one or two calls to make,' he said cheerfully.

'Oh hell,' said the fat man.

'There's a phone outside physio. Try there,' said a passing nurse.

'I'll try there,' said the fat man.

Midgley sat on.

'Hello,' said the young man brightly. 'Dorothy? You're a grandma.' He looked at Midgley while he was talking, but without seeing him.

'A grandma,' he shouted. 'Yes!' There was a pause. 'Guess,' said the young man and listened. 'No,' he said. 'Girl. Seven and a half pounds. 5.35. Both doing well. I'm ringing everybody. Bye, Grandma.'

Midgley half rose as the young man put the receiver back, but sat back as he consulted a bit of paper then picked it up again and dialled.

'Hello, Neil. Hi. You're an uncle . . . You're an un-cle. Today. Just now. 5.35. Well, guess.' He waited. 'No. Girl. No. I'm over the moon. So you can tell Christine she's an aunty. Yes, a little cousin for Jose-phine. How's it feel to be an uncle? . . . Bye.'

Midgley got up and stood waiting. The young man took another coin and dialled again. It was a way of breaking news that could be adapted for exits as well as entrances, thought Midgley.

'Hello, Margaret. You're a widow. A widow . . . This afternoon. Half-past two . . . How's it feel to be bereaved?'

'Betty,' said the young man. 'Congratulations.'

'You're an aunty. Aunty Betty. I won't ask you to guess,' he went on hurriedly. 'It's a girl. Susan's over the moon. And I am.'

With each call his enthusiasm had definitely de-creased. Midgley reflected that this baby was well on the way to being a bore and it was only a couple of hours old.

'I'm just telephoning with the glad tidings. Bye, Aunty.'

The proud father put a new pile of coins on the box and Midgley was moved to intervene.

'Could I just make one call?'

'Won't it wait,' said the young man. 'I was here first. I'm a father.'

'I'm a son,' said Midgley. 'My father's dying.'

'There's no need to take that tone,' said the young man, stepping out of the helmet. 'You should have spoken up. There's a phone outside physio.'

Midgley listened to the phone ringing along the passage at his father's brother's house.

'Uncle Ernest? It's Denis. Dad's been taken poorly.'

'You mean Frank?' said his uncle.

'Yes. Dad. He's had a stroke,' said Midgley. 'And a fall. And now he's got pneumonia.' Somehow he felt he ought to have selected two out of three, not laid everything on the line first go off.

'Oh dear, oh dear, oh dear,' said his uncle. 'Our Frank.'

'Can you ring round and tell anybody who might want to come. The doctor says he won't last the night.'

'From here? Me ring?'

It started pipping.

'Yes. I'm in a box. There are people waiting.'

'You never know,' said the young man. 'They can work miracles nowadays.'

. . .

'THIS IS WHAT I'd call an industrial lift,' said Uncle Ernest, tapping the wall with his strong boot. 'It's not an ordinary passenger lift, this. It's as big as our sitting room.'

It stopped and a porter slid a trolley in beside Midgley. A woman looked up at him and smiled faintly.

'Is it working?' said the porter. The little head closed its eyes.

'We've just had a nice jab and now we're going for a ta ta.'

Behind a glass panel Midgley watched the concrete floors pass.

'It's very solidly constructed,' said Uncle Ernest, looking at the floor. 'These are overlapping steel plates. We can still do it when we try.'

'Let the dog see the rabbit,' said the porter as the lift stopped.

'This is six,' said Midgley.

'Every floor looks the same to me,' said his uncle.

'Did you ring our Hartley?' Hartley was Uncle Ernest's son and a chartered accountant.

'He's coming as soon as he can get away.'

'Was he tied up?'

He had been.

'Secretary was it? Was he in a meeting? I'd like to know what they are, these meetings he's always in, that he can't speak to his father. "Excuse me, I have to speak to my father." That's no disgrace, is it? "I won't be a moment, my dad's on the line." Who's going to take offence at that? Who are they, in these meetings? Don't they have fathers? I thought fathers were universal. Instead of which I have to make an appointment to see my own son. Sons, fathers, you shouldn't need appointments. You should get straight through. You weren't like that with your dad. Frank thought the world of you.'

They were going down the long corridor again.

'I came on the diesel,' said Uncle Ernest. He was lame in one leg.

'I go all over. I went to York last week. Saw the railway museum. There's stock in there I drove. Museum in my own lifetime. I'll tell you one thing.'

They stopped.

'What,' said Midgley.

'I wouldn't like to have to polish this floor.'

They resumed.

'You still schoolteaching?'

Midgley nodded.

'Pleased your dad, did that. Though it won't be much of a salary. You'd have been better off doing something in our Hartley's line. He's up there in the £30,000 bracket now. She was talking about a swimming pool.'

They stopped at the entrance to Intensive Care while his uncle stood, one arm stretched out to the wall, taking the weight off his leg.

'Is your Aunty Kitty here?'

'Yes.'

'I thought she would be. Where no vultures fly.'

AUNTY KITTY GOT UP and did her 'I am too upset to speak' act. 'Hello, Kitty,' said Ernest.

'I always thought I should be the first, Ernest.'

'Well you still might be. He's not dead yet.'

'Go in, Ernest.' She dabbed her nose. 'Go in.'

Uncle Ernest stood by his brother's bed. Then he sat down.

'This is summat fresh for you, Frank,' he said. 'You were always such a bouncer.' He stood up and leaned over the bed to look closer at the bleeps on the scanner. They were bouncing merrily. A nurse looked in.

'You're not to touch that.'

'I was just interested.'

'He's very ill.'

She paused for a moment, came further into the room and looked at the scanner. She looked at Uncle Ernest (though not, he noticed, at Frank) and went out.

'It's all mechanised now,' he said.

There was no sound in the room. The brothers had never had much to say to each other at the best of times. Without there being any animosity, they felt easier in the presence of a third party; alone they embarrassed each other. It was still the case, even though one of them was unconscious, and Uncle Ernest got up, thankful to be able to go.

'Ta-ra then, butt,' he said.

And waited.

He wanted to pat his brother's hand.

'I went to York last week,' he said. 'It hasn't changed much. They haven't spoiled it like they have Leeds. Though there's one of these precinct things. It's the first time I've been since we were lads. We went over on our bikes once.' Instead of touching his brother's hand he jogged his foot in farewell, just as the nurse was coming in.

'He's *very* ill,' she said, smoothing the coverlet over his brother's feet. 'And this is delicate equipment.'

'I went in,' she said in the canteen later, 'and there was one of them pulling a patient's leg about. He had hold of his foot. It's an uphill battle.'

UNCLE ERNEST'S SON Hartley came with his wife Jean and their children, Mark (14) and Elizabeth (10). Hartley hated hospitals, hence his demand for full family back-up. He was actually surprised that Mark had condescended to come: a big 14, Mark had long since passed beyond parental control and only appeared with the family on state occasions. The truth was that Miss Pollock, who took him for Religious Knowledge and who was known to be fucking at least one of the sixth form, had pointed out only last week how rare were the opportunities these days of seeing a dead person, and thus of acquiring a real perspective on the human condition. Mark was hoping this visit might gain him some status in the eyes of Miss Pollock. Sensitive to the realities of birth and death, he hoped to be the next candidate for 'bringing out'.

They were all going up in the lift.

'Think on,' said Hartley. 'It's quite likely your

grandad'll be here. I don't want you asking for all sorts in front of him.'

'No,' said his wife. 'We don't want him saying you're spoiled.'

'Though you are spoiled,' said Hartley.

'Whose fault is that?' said Jean.

The steel doors folded back to reveal Denis saying goodbye to Uncle Ernest.

'Now then, Dad,' said Hartley. 'Hello, Denis. This is a bad do.'

Jean kissed the old man.

'Give your grandad a kiss, Elizabeth.'

The child did so.

'Come on, Mark.'

'I don't kiss now,' said the boy.

'You kiss your grandad,' said Hartley and the boy did so and a nurse, passing, looked.

'How is he?' said Hartley.

'Dying,' said his father. 'Sinking fast.'

'Oh dear, oh dear, oh dear,' said Hartley, who had hoped it would be all over by now.

'And how've you been keeping?' said Jean, brightly.

'Champion,' said Uncle Ernest. 'Is that one of them new watches?' He took Mark's wrist.

'He had to save up for it,' said Jean. 'You had to save up for it, didn't you, Mark?'

Mark nodded.

'He didn't,' said the little girl.

'I never had a watch till I was 21,' said the old man. 'Of course, they're 21 at 18 now, aren't they?'

Denis pressed the button for the lift.

'We'd better get along to the ward if he's that critical,' said Jean.

'I've had the receiver in my hand to give you a ring once or twice,' said Hartley as they waited for the lift, 'then a client's come in.'

'I was thinking of going to Barnard Castle next week,' said Ernest.

'Whatever for?' said Jean, kissing him goodbye.

'I've never been.' He shook Denis's hand. The lift doors closed. Hartley and his family walked ahead of Midgley down the long corridor.

'I'll give you such a clatter when I get you home, young lady,' Jean was saying. 'He did save up.'

'Only a week,' said the child.

'When we get there,' said Hartley, 'we want to go in in twos. All together would be too much of a strain.'

'What's he doing going to Barnard Castle?' said Jean.

'He can't be short of money taking himself off to Barnard Castle.'

Midgley caught them up.

'You'd no need all to come,' he said. 'I wouldn't let Joyce bring ours.'

'They wanted to come,' said Jean. 'Our Mark did especially, didn't you Mark?'

'It's more handy for us, anyway,' said Hartley. 'What did we do before the M62?'

Mark was disappointed. The old man was quite plainly breathing. He could quite easily have been asleep. He wasn't even white.

'He's not my uncle, is he, Dad?'

'He's my uncle. He's your great-uncle.'

Hartley was looking at the screen.

'You see this screen, Mark? It's monitoring his heartbeats.'

Mark didn't look, but said wearily, 'I know, Dad.'

'I was only telling you.'

Hartley touched the screen where the beep was flickering.

'You want to learn, don't you?' his father said as they came out.

'Dad.' The boy stopped. 'We made one of those at school.'

Jean now led little Elizabeth in. ('Bless her,' said Aunty Kitty.)

They stood hand in hand by the bedside, and Jean bent down and kissed him.

'Do you want me to kiss him?' said the child.

'No. I don't think so, love,' and she rubbed her lips with her hanky where they had touched him.

'Are you crying, Mam?' said the child.

'Yes.'

The little girl looked up at her.

'There aren't any tears.'

'You can cry without tears,' said her mother, looking at the monitor. 'You can cry more without tears.'

'I can't,' said the child. 'How do you do it, Mam?'

'It comes when you're grown up.'

'I want to be able to do it now.'

'Listen, I'll give you such a smack in a minute,' said her mother. 'He's dying.'

Elizabeth began to cry.

'There, love.' Her mother hugged her. 'He doesn't feel it.'

'I'm not crying because of him,' said the child. 'I'm crying because of you.'

'I wouldn't have another Cortina,' said Hartley. 'I used to swear by Cortinas. No longer.'

Midgley was watching an Indian man and his son sat in the corner. The father's face ran with tears as he hugged the child to him so that he seemed in danger of smothering the boy.

'You still got the VW?'

Midgley nodded.

'I think I might go in for a Peugeot,' said Hartley. 'A 604. Buy British.' There was a pause, and he added: 'He was a nice old chap.'

Jean and Elizabeth returned and Mark, who had been in the corridor, came in to ask how long they were stopping.

Hartley looked at Jean.

'I think we ought to wait just a bit, don't you, darling?'

'Oh yes,' said Jean. 'Just in case.'

Aunty Kitty came in. 'I've just had one coffee and a wagon wheel and it was 45p. And it's all supposed to be voluntary.'

'There isn't a disco, is there?' said Mark.

'Disco?' said Jean. 'Disco? This is a hospital.'

'Well. Leisure facilities. Facilities for visitors. Killing time.'

'Listen,' Jean hissed. 'Your Uncle Denis's father is dying and you talk about discos.'

'It's all right,' said Midgley.

'Here, go get yourself a coffee,' said Hartley, giving him a pound. Aunty Kitty looked away.

HARTLEY AND HIS family were going. They were congregated outside the lift.

'You'll wait, I expect,' said Hartley.

'Oh yes,' said Midgley, 'I want to be here.'

'You want to make it plain at this stage you don't want him resuscitating.'

'That's if he doesn't want him resuscitating,' said Jean. 'You don't know.'

'I wouldn't want my dad resuscitating,' said Hartley.

'Denis might, mightn't you Denis?'

'No,' said Midgley.

'You often don't get the choice,' said Hartley. 'They'll resuscitate anybody given half a chance. Shove them on these life-support machines. It's all to do with cost-effectiveness. They invest in this expensive equipment then they feel they have to use it.' He pumped the lift button. 'My guess is that it'll be at four in the morning, the crucial time. That's when life's at its lowest ebb, the early hours.'

'Miracles do happen, of course,' said Jean. 'I was reading about these out-of-body experiences. Have you read about them, Denis? It's where very sick people float in the air above their own bodies. Personally,' Jean kissed Midgley, 'I think it won't be long before science will be coming round to an after-life. Bye bye. I wish it had been on a happier occasion.'

Midgley went down the long corridor.

'MONEY'S NO GOOD,' said Aunty Kitty. 'Look at President Kennedy. They've been a tragic family.'

The Indians slept, the little son laid with his head in the father's lap.

An orderly came in and tidied the magazines, emptied the waste-bin and took away a vase of flowers.

'Oxygen,' he said as he went out.

'The Collingwoods got back from Corfu,' said Aunty Kitty. 'They said they enjoyed it but they wouldn't go a second time.'

It was after ten and Midgley had assumed she was going to stay the night when she suddenly got up.

'If I go now I can get the twenty-to,' she said. 'I'll just get back before they're turning out. I never go upstairs. It's just asking for it.'

'I'll walk down with you,' said Midgley.

She tiptoed elaborately past the sleeping immigrants, favouring them with a benevolent smile.

'They've got feelings the same as us,' she whispered. 'They're fond of their families. More so, probably.' They came out into the corridor. 'But then they're less advanced than we are.'

He phoned Joyce.

She and Colin were watching a programme about dolphins that had been introduced by the Duke of Edinburgh. Her mother was asleep with her mouth open.

'What're you doing?' asked Midgley.

'Nothing. Colin's watching a programme about dolphins. How is he?'

Midgley told her.

'I've got to stay,' he finished.

'Why? You've done all that's necessary. Nobody's going to blame you.'

Midgley saw that somebody had written on the wall 'Pray for me.' A wag had added 'OK.'

'I must be here when he goes,' said Midgley. 'You can understand that.'

'I understand you,' she said. 'It's not love. It's not affection.' Colin looked up. 'It's yourself.'

She put the phone down.

'Dad?' said Colin.

She turned the television off. 'He's hanging on.'

'Who?'

'Your grandad.' She got up. 'Wake up Mother. Time for bed.'

MIDGLEY WENT BACK and sat with his father. While he had been out the night nurse had come on. She was a plump girl, dark, less pert than the others, and, he thought, more human. Actually she was just dirty. The hair wasn't gathered properly under her cap and there was a ladder in her stocking. She straightened the bedclothes, bending over the inert form so that her behind was inches from Midgley's face. Midgley decided it wasn't deliberate.

'Am I in the way?' he asked.

'No,' she said. 'Why? Stop there.'

She looked at the television monitor for a minute or two, counting the jumps with her watch. Then she smiled and went out. Five minutes later she was back with a cup of tea.

'No sugar,' said Midgley.

'May I?' she said and put both lumps in her mouth.

'Slack tonight,' she said. 'Still it just needs one drunken driver.'

Midgley closed his eyes.

'I thought you were going to be a bit of company,'

she said. 'You're tired out.' She fetched a pillow and they went out into the waiting room. The Indians had gone.

'Lie down,' she said. 'I'll wake you if anything happens.'

Around five an alarm went off, and there were two deaths in quick succession. Midgley slept on. At eight he woke.

'You can't lie down,' said a voice. 'You're not supposed to lie down.' It was a clean, fresh nurse.

Two women he had not seen before sat watching him.

'The nurse said she'd wake me up.'

'What nurse?'

'If anything happened to my father.'

'Whose is that pillow?'

'Midgley. Mr Midgley.'

'It's a hospital pillow.' She took it, and went back inside to her desk.

'Midgley.' Her finger ran down the list. 'No change. But don't lie down. It's not fair on other people.'

Midgley went and looked at his father. No change was right. He felt old and dirty. He had not shaved and there was a cold sore starting on his lip. But with his father there was no change. Still clean. Still pink. Still breathing. The dot skipped on. He walked out to the car park where he had left his van and wondered if he dared risk going out to buy a razor.

He went back in search of the doctor.

He cut across the visitors' car park, empty now except for his van, and took a path round the outside of the hospital that he thought would take him round to the entrance. The buildings were long and low and set in the hillside. They were done in identical units, every ward the same. He was passing a ward that seemed just like his father's except where his father should have been a woman was just putting her breast to a baby's mouth. A nurse came to the window and stared at him. He looked away hurriedly and walked on, but not so quickly as to leave her with the impression he had been watching. She was still staring at him as he turned the corner. He experienced a feeling of relief if not quite homecoming when he saw he was now outside Intensive Care. He picked out his father's room, saw the carnations on the window sill and the head and shoulders of a nurse. She was obviously looking at the bed. She moved back towards the window to make room for someone else. Midgley stood on tiptoe to try and see what was happening. He thought there was someone else there in a white coat. The room was full of people.

Midgley ran round the unit trying to find a way in.
There was a door at the end of the building with an
empty corridor beyond. It was locked. He ran up to
the path again, then cut down across the bank through
some young trees to try another door. A man on the
telephone watched him sliding down then put one
phone down and picked up another. Midgley ran on
and suddenly was in a muddy flower bed among
bushes and evergreens. It was the garden around the
entrance to the Reception Area. Upstairs he ran past
the startled nurse at the desk and into his father's room.
Nobody spoke. There was an atmosphere of reverence.

'Is he dead?' said Midgley. 'Has he gone?' He was
panting. An older woman in blue turned round.
'Dead? Certainly not. I am the matron. And look at
your shoes.'

Behind the matron Midgley caught a glimpse of his
father. As a nurse bustled him out Midgley struggled
to look back. He was sure his father was smiling.

'I've just been to spend a penny,' said Aunty Kitty.
'When you consider it's a hospital the toilets are nothing to write home about. Look at your shoes.'

She was beginning to settle in, had brought a flask,
sandwiches, knitting.

'I know Frank,' she said, looking at *Country Life*.

'He'll make a fight of it. I wouldn't thank you for a place in Bermuda.'

Midgley went to the gents to have a wash. He got some toilet paper and stood by the basins wiping the mud off his boots. He was stood with the muddy paper in his hands when an orderly came in, looked at the paper then looked at him incredulously, shook his head and went into a cubicle saying: 'The fucking public. The fucking dirty bastard public.'

Midgley went down to ring his Uncle Ernest on the phone outside physio. A youngish woman was just dialling.

'Cyril. It's . . .' She held the mouthpiece away from her mouth and the earpiece from her ear. 'It's Vi. Vi. I am speaking into it. Mum's had her op. No. She's had it. Had it this morning first thing. She's not come round yet, but I spoke to the sister and apparently she's fine. FINE. And the sister says . . .' She dropped her voice. 'It wasn't what we thought. It wasn't what we thought. No. So there's no need to worry.' She ran her finger over the acoustic headboard behind the phone, fingering the holes. 'No. Completely clear. Well I think it's good news, don't you? The sister said the surgeon is the best. Mr Caldecott. People pay thousands to have him. Anyway I'm so relieved. Aren't you? Yes. Bye.'

As Midgley took the phone she took out her handkerchief and rubbed it over her lips, and safely outside the hospital, her ear.

UNCLE ERNEST had said on the phone that if this was going to go on he wasn't sure he could run to the fares, but he turned up in the late afternoon along with Hartley.

He went and sat with his brother for a bit, got down and looked under the bed and figured out how the mechanism worked that lifted and lowered it and finally stood up and said, 'Gillo, Frank,' which was what he used to say when they went out cycling between the wars. It meant 'hurry up'.

'It's Frank all over,' said Aunty Kitty, 'going down fighting. He loved life.'

There were a couple of newcomers in the waiting room, an oldish couple.

'It's their eldest daughter,' whispered Aunty Kitty. 'She was just choosing some new curtains in Schofields. Collapsed. Suspected brain haemorrhage. Their other son's a vet.'

They trailed down the long corridor to the lift.

'It's a wonder to me,' said Uncle Ernest, 'how your Aunty Kitty's managed to escape strangulation all these years. Was he coloured, this doctor?'

'Which?' said Midgley.

'That said he was on his last legs.'

Midgley reluctantly admitted he was.

'That explains it,' said the old railwayman.

'Dad,' said Hartley.

'What does that mean, "Dad"?' said his father.

'It means I'm vice-chairman of the community relations council. It means we've got one in the office and he's a tip-top accountant. It means we all have to live with one another in this world.' He pumped the button of the lift.

'I'll not come again,' said Uncle Ernest. 'It gets morbid.'

'We've just got to play it by ear,' said Hartley.

'You won't have this performance with me,' said the old man. 'Come once and have done.'

'Shall I drop you?' said Hartley as the doors opened.

'I don't want you to go out of your way.'

'No, but shall I drop you?'

'Press G,' said Uncle Ernest.

The lift doors closed.

. . .

MIDGLEY WAS SITTING with his father when the
plump night nurse came on.

'I wondered if you'd be on tonight.' He read her
tab. 'Nurse Lightfoot.'

'Waiting for me, were you? No change.' She took
a tissue and wiped the old man's mouth. 'He doesn't
want to leave us, does he?' She picked up the vase of
carnations from the window sill. 'Oxygen,' she said
and took them outside.

Later, when she had made him a cup of tea and
Aunty Kitty had gone home for the second night, he
was sitting at the bedside but got up when she started
to give his father a bed bath.

'You're like one another.'

He stared out of the window, even moved to avoid
seeing the reflection.

'No,' he said.

'You are. It's a compliment. He has a nice face.' She
sponged under his arms.

'What are you?' she said.

'How do you mean?' He turned just as she had
folded back the sheets and was sponging between his
legs. Quickly he looked out of the window again.

'What do you do?'

'Teacher. I'm a teacher.' He wanted to go and sit in the waiting room.

'What was he?'

'Plumber.'

'He's got lovely hands. Real ladies' hands.'

And it was true. She had finished and the soft white hands of his father lay over the sheet.

'That happens in hospitals. People's hands change.' She held his father's hand. Midgley wondered if he could ask her to hold his. Probably. She looked even more of a mess than the night before.

'Is there anything you want to ask?'

'Yes,' said Midgley.

'If there is, doctor'll be round in a bit.'

It was a different doctor. Not Indian. Fair, curly-haired and aged not much more than fourteen.

'His condition certainly hasn't deteriorated,' the child said. 'On the other hand,' he glanced boyishly at the chart, 'it can't be said to have improved.'

Midgley wondered if he had ever had his ears pierced.

'I don't know that there's any special point in waiting. You've done your duty.' He gave him a winning smile and had Midgley been standing closer would probably have put his hand on his arm as he had been taught to do.

'After all,' he was almost conspiratorial, 'he doesn't know you're here.'

'I don't think he's dying,' said Midgley.

'Living, dying,' said the boy and shrugged. The words meant the same thing.

'You do want your father to live?' He turned towards the nurse and pulled a little face.

'I was told he wasn't going to last long. I live in Hull.'

'Our task is to make them last as long as possible.' The pretty boy looked at his watch. 'We've no obligation to get them off on time.'

'Some of them seem to think we're British Rail,' the doctor remarked to a nurse in the small hours when they were having a smoke after sexual intercourse.

'I don't like 15-year-old doctors, that's all,' said Midgley. 'I'm old enough to be his father. Does nobody else wait? Does nobody else feel they have to be here?'

'Why not go sleep in your van? I can give you a pillow and things.' She was eating a toffee. 'I'll send somebody down to the car park if anything happens.'

'What do you do all day?' asked Midgley.

'Sleep.' She was picking a bit of toffee from her tooth. 'I generally surface around three.'

'Maybe we could have a coffee. If he's unchanged.'

'OK.'

She smiled. He had forgotten how easy it was.

'I'll just have another squint at my dad.'

He came back. 'Come and look. I think he's moved.'

She ran ahead of him into the room. The old man lay back on the pillows, a shaded light by the bed.

'You had me worried for a moment,' she said. 'It's all right.'

'No. His face has changed.'

She switched on the lamp over the bed, the light so sudden and bright that that alone might have made the old man flinch. But nothing moved.

'It's just that he seemed to be smiling.'

'You're tired,' she said, put her hand against his face and switched out the light.

Midgley switched it on again.

'If you look long enough at him you'll see a smile.'

'If you look long enough,' she said, walking out of the room, 'you'll see anything you want.'

Midgley stood for a moment in the darkened room,

wishing he had kissed her when he'd had the chance. He went out to look for her but there had been a pile-up on the M62 and all hell was about to break loose.

'WHAT DO YOU DO ALL DAY?' said his wife on the phone. 'Sit in the waiting room. Sit in his room. Walk round the hospital.'

'Don't they mind?'

'Not if they're going to die.'

'Is he, though?' said his wife, watching her mother who had taken up her station on the chair by the door, holding her bag on her knees, preparatory to going to bed. 'It seems a long time.' The old lady was falling asleep. Once she had slipped right off that chair and cracked her head on the sideboard. That had been a hospital do.

'I can't talk. Mum's waiting to go up. She's crying out for a bath. I'm just going to have to steel myself.' The handbag slipped to the floor.

'I need a bath,' said Midgley.

'Go over to your dad's,' said his wife. 'Mum's falling over. Bye.'

'What am I doing sat on this seat?' said her mother, as she got her up. 'I never sit on this seat. I don't think I've ever sat on this seat before.'

. . .

IN THE MORNING Midgley was woken by Nurse Lightfoot banging on the steamed-up window of the van. It was seven o'clock.

'I'm just going off,' she was mouthing through the glass.

He wound down the window.

'I'm just coming off. Isn't it a grand morning? I'm going to have a big fried breakfast then go to bed. I'll see you at teatime. You look terrible.'

Midgley looked at himself in the driving mirror, then started up the van and drove after her, hooting.

'You're not supposed to hoot,' she said. 'It's a hospital.'

'I forgot to ask you. How's my dad?'

'No change.' She waved and ran down a grass bank towards the nurses' flats. 'No change.'

His dad lived where he had lived once, at the end of a terrace of redbrick back-to-back houses. It was an end house, as his mother had always been careful to point out. It gave them one more window, which was nice, only kids used the end wall to play football against, which wasn't. His dad used to heave himself up from the fireside and go out to them, night after night. He let himself in with the key he had had since he was 14. 'You're 21 now,' his mother had said.

The house was neat and clean and cold. He looked for some sign of interrupted activity, even a chair out of place, some clue as to what his father had been doing when the blow fell. But there was nothing. He had a home help. She had probably tidied up. He put the kettle on, before having a shave. He knew where everything was. His dad's razor on the shelf above the sink, a shaving brush worn down to a stub and a half-used packet of Seven O'Clock blades. He scrubbed away the caked rust from the razor ('Your dad doesn't care,' said his mother) and put in a new blade. He had never gone in for shaving soap. Puritan soap they always bought, green Puritan soap. Then having shaved he took his shirt off to wash in the same sequence he had seen his father follow every night when he came in from work. Then, thinking of the coming afternoon, he did something he had never seen his father do, take off his trousers and his pants to wash his cock. He smelled his shirt. It stank. Naked, white and shivering he went through the neat sitting room and up the narrow stairs and stood on the cold lino of his parents' bedroom looking at himself in the dressing-table mirror. On top of the dressing-table, stood on little lace mats, was a toilet set. A round glass jar for a powder-puff, a pin tray, a cut-glass dish with a small pinnacle in the middle, for rings, and a celluloid-backed mirror and hairbrush. Items that had never had a practical use, but which had lain there in their appointed place for forty years.

He opened the dressing-table drawer, and found a new shirt still in its packet. They had given it to his father as a Christmas present two years before. He put it on, carefully extracting all the pins and putting them in the cut-glass dish. He looked for pants and found a pair that were old, baggy and gone a bit yellow. Some socks. Nothing quite fitted. He was smaller than his father. These days it was generally the other way round. He went downstairs, through into the scullery to polish his shoes. He remembered the brushes, the little brush to put the polish on which as a child he had always thought of as bad, the big noble brush that brought out the shine. He stood on the hearthrug and saw himself in the mirror, ready as if for a funeral, and sat down on the settee about to weep when he realised it was not his father's funeral he was imagining but his own. On the end of the tiled mantelpiece of which his mother had been so proud when they had had it put in in 1953 (a crime getting rid of that beautiful range, Joyce always said) was his dad's pipe. It was still half full of charred tobacco. He put it back but rolling over it fell on to the hearth. He stooped to pick it up and was his father suddenly, bending down, falling and lying there two days with the pipe under his hand. He dashed out of the house and drove wildly back to the hospital.

'No change,' said the nurse wearily (they were beginning to think he was mad). But if there was no change at least the old man didn't seem to be smiling.

'I'm wearing your shirt, Dad,' Midgley said. 'The one we gave you for Christmas. I hope that's all right. It doesn't really suit me, but I think that's why Joyce bought it. She said it didn't suit me but it would suit you.'

A nurse came in.

'They tell you to talk,' said Midgley. 'I read it in an article in the *Reader's Digest*,' (and as if this gave it added force), 'it was in the waiting room.'

The nurse sniffed. 'They say the same thing about plants,' she said, putting the carnations back on the window sill. 'I think it's got past that stage.'

. . .

MIDGLEY WAS SITTING on the divan bed in Nurse Lightfoot's room in the nurses' quarters. The rooms were light and modern like the hospital. She was sitting by the electric fire with one bar on. There was a Snoopy poster on the wall.

'People are funny about nurses,' she said. 'Men.' She took a bite of her bun. They were muesli buns. 'You say you're a nurse and their whole attitude changes. Do you know what I mean?'

'No,' lied Midgley.

'I notice it at parties particularly. They ask you what you do, you say you're a nurse and next minute they've got you on the floor. Perfectly ordinary people turn into wild beasts.' She switched another bar on.

'I've given up saying I'm a nurse for that reason.'

'What do you say you are?' asked Midgley. He wondered whether he would be better placed if he went over to the fire or he got her to come over to the bed.

'I say I'm a sales representative. I don't mean you,' she said. 'You're obviously not like that. Course you've got other things on your mind at the moment.'

'Like what?'

'Your dad.'

'Oh yes.'

The duty nurse had been instructed to ring if there was any sign of a crisis.

'He is lovely,' she said, through mouthfuls of bun. 'I do understand the way you feel about him.'

'Do you?' said Midgley. 'That's nice.'

'Old people have their own particular attraction. He's almost sexy.'

Midgley stood up suddenly.

She picked something out of her mouth.

'Was your cake gritty?'

'No,' said Midgley, sitting down again.

'Mine was. Mine was a bit gritty.'

'It was probably meant to be gritty,' said Midgley, looking at his watch.

'No. It was more gritty than that.'

'What would you say,' asked Midgley, as he carefully examined a small stain on the bedcover, 'what would you say if I asked you to go to bed.'

'Now?' she asked, extracting another piece of grit or grain.

'If you like.' He made it sound as if she had made the suggestion.

'I can't now.' She gathered up the cups and plates.

'Why not? You're not on till seven.'

'It's Wednesday. I'm on early turn.' She wondered if he was going to turn into a wild beast.

'Tomorrow then?'

'Tomorrow would be better. Though of course it all depends.'

'What on?'

She was shocked.

'Your father. He may not be here tomorrow.'

'That's true,' said Midgley, getting up. He kissed her fairly formally.

'Anyway,' she smiled. 'Fingers crossed.'

MIDGLEY SAT by his father's bed and watched the dot skipping on the screen.

'Hold on, Dad,' he muttered. 'Hold on.'

There was no change.

Before going down to sleep in the van he telephoned home. It was his son who answered. Joyce was upstairs with her mother.

'Could you ask her to come to the phone, please,' said Midgley. The 'please' was somehow insulting. He heard brief shouting.

'She can't,' said Colin. 'Gran's in the bath. Mum can't leave her. What do you want?'

'You go up and watch her while I speak to your Mum.'

'Dad.' The boy's voice was slow with weary out-rage. 'Dad. She's in the bath. She's no clothes on. I don't want to see her.'

He heard more distant shouting.

'Mum says if she can get a granny-sitter she may come over to see Grandad.'

'Colin.' Midgley was suddenly urgent. 'Colin. Are you still there?'

'Sure.' (Midgley hated that.)

'Tell her not to do that. Do you hear? Tell her there's no need to come over. Go on, tell her.'

'I'll tell her when she comes down.'

'No,' said Midgley. 'Now. I know you. Go up and tell her now.'

The phone was put down and he could hear Colin bellowing up the stairs. He came back.

'I told her. Is that all?'

'No,' said Midgley. 'Haven't you forgotten some-thing? How's Grandad? Haven't you forgotten that? Well it's nice of you to ask, Colin. He's about the same, Colin, thank you.'

'How was your grandad?' said Joyce, coming downstairs with a wet towel and a bundle of her mother's underclothes.

'About the same,' said Colin.

'And your dad?'

'No change.'

THAT NIGHT MIDGLEY dreamed it was morning when the door opened and his father got into the van.

'I didn't know you drove, Dad,' he said as they were going into town. 'When did you learn?'

'Just before I died.'

His mother, as a girl, met them outside the Town Hall.

'What a spanking van, Frank,' she said. 'Move up, Denis, let me sit next to your dad.'

The three of them sat in a row until he saw her hand was on his father's leg, when suddenly he was in a field alone with his mother.

'What a grand field,' she said. 'It's spotless.'

He was a little boy and she was in a white frock, and some terrible threat had just been lifted. Then he looked behind him and saw something much worse. On the edge of the field, ready to engulf them, was an enormous slag heap, glinting black and shiny in the sun. His mother hadn't seen it and chattered on how lovely this field was and slipping nearer came this terrible hill. Someone ran down the slope, waving his arms, a figure big and filthy, a miner, a coalman. He slid down beside them.

'Oh,' she said placidly, 'here's your father,' and he sat down beside her, coal and muck all over her white frock.

Then they were walking through Leeds Market. It was Sunday and the stalls were empty and shuttered. It was also a church and they walked up through the market to the choir screen. It was in the form of a board announcing Arrivals and Departures, slips of board clicking over with names on them, only instead of Arrivals and Departures it was headed Births and Deaths. Midgley wandered off while his parents sat looking at the board. Then his mam got up and kissed his dad, and went backwards through the screen just before the gates were drawn across. Midgley tried to run down the church and couldn't. He was shouting 'Mam. Mam.' Eventually he got to the gates and started shaking them, but she had gone. He turned to look at his father who shook his head slowly and turned away. Midgley went on rattling the gates then someone was shaking the van. It was Nurse Lightfoot waking him up. 'You can call me Valery,' she chanted as she ran off to her big breakfast.

Later that morning Midgley went in to see his father to find a smartish middle-aged woman sat by the bed. She was holding his father's hand.

'Is it Denis?' she said without getting up.

'Yes.'

'I'm Alice Dugdale. Did he tell you about me?'

'No.'

'He wouldn't, being him. He's an old bugger. Aren't you?'

She shook the inert hand. She was in her fifties, Midgley decided, very confident and done up to the nines. His mother would have called her common. She looked like the wife of a prosperous licensee.

'He told me about you,' she said. 'He never stopped telling me about you. It's a sad sight.'

The nurse had said his father was a bit better this morning.

'His condition's stabilised,' said Midgley.

'Yes, she said that to me, the little slut. What does she know?' She looked at him. 'You're a bit scruffy.' She stood up and smoothed down her skirt. 'I've come from Southport.' She took the carnations from the vase and put them in the waste-bin. 'A depressing flower, carnations,' she said. 'I prefer freesias. I'm a widow,' she said. 'A rich widow. Shall we have a meander round? No sense in stopping here.' She kissed his father on the forehead. 'His lordship's not got much to contribute. Bye bye chick.'

She swept through the waiting room with Midgley in her wake. Aunty Kitty open-mouthed got up and went out to watch them going down the corridor.

'That'll be your Aunty Kitty, I take it.' She said it loudly enough for her to hear.

'It is, yes,' said Denis, glancing back and smiling weakly. 'Do you know her?'

'No, thank God. Though she probably knows me.'

They found a machine and had some coffee. She took a silver flask from her bag.

'Do you want some of this in it?'

'No thanks,' said Midgley.

'I'd better,' she said. 'I've driven from Southport. I wanted to marry your dad only he said no. I had too much money. My husband left me very nicely placed. He was a leading light in the soft furnishing trade. Frank would have felt beholden, you see. That was your dad all over. Still you know what he was like.'

Midgley was no longer sure he did.

'How do you mean?' he said.

'He always had to be the one, did Frank. The one who did the good turns, the one who paid out, the one who sacrificed. You couldn't do anything for him. I had all this money and he wouldn't even let me take him to Scarborough. We used to go sit in Roundhay Park. Roundhay Park!'

A woman went by, learning to use crutches.

'We could have been in Tenerife.'

Midgley was glad to have at least this aspect of his father's character confirmed.

'I didn't want to let him down,' said Midgley. 'That's why I've been waiting. He wants me to let him down, I know.'

'Poor soul,' she said, looking at the woman struggling down the corridor.

'What was your mam like?'

'She was lovely,' said Midgley.

'She must have had him taped. She looks a grand woman. He's showed me photographs.' She took out her compact and made up her face. 'I'll go back and have another look. Then I've got to get over to a Round Table in Harrogate. Killed two birds with one stone for me, this trip.'

. . .

'YOUR MOTHER'D not been dead a year,' sniffed Aunty Kitty. 'I was shocked.'

'I'm not shocked.'

'You're a man.'

'It wasn't like your dad. She's a cheek showing her face.'

'I'm rather pleased,' said Midgley.

'That hair's dyed,' said Aunty Kitty, but it was a last despairing throw. 'They're sending him downstairs to-morrow. He must be on the mend.' The drama was about to go out of her life. 'I only hope when he does come round he's not a vegetable.'

'I'VE TOLD SHIRLEY to ring if anything happens,' Valery said. 'Not that it will. His chest is better. His heart is better. He's simply unconscious now.'

Midgley was brushing his teeth.

'I'm looking forward to him coming round.' She raised her voice above the running tap. 'I long to know what his voice is like.'

'What?' said Midgley turning off the tap.

'I long to know what his voice is like.'

'Oh,' said Midgley. 'Yes.' And turned the tap on again.

'I think I know what it's like,' she said. 'I'd just like to have it confirmed.'

'You don't seem to like talking about your father,' she said as she unzipped her skirt. 'Nice shirt.'

'Yes,' said Midgley. 'It's one of Dad's.'

'I like it.'

He went and had a pee and while he was out she took the receiver off the phone and put a cushion over it. When he came back she was already in bed.

'Hello,' he said, getting in and lying beside her. 'It's a bit daft is this.'

'Why?' she said. 'It happens all the time.'

'Yes,' said Midgley. 'So I'm told.'

They kissed.

'I ought to have done more of this.'

'What?'

'This,' said Midgley. 'This is going to be the rule from now on. I've got a lot of catching up to do.'

He ran his hand between her thighs.

'It's the nick of time.'

'First time I've heard it called that.'

'I hope this isn't one of those private beds,' said Midgley. 'I'm opposed to that on principle.'

'You've never asked me if I was married,' she said.

'You're a nurse. That puts you in a different category.' There was a pause. 'Are you married?'

'He's on an oil rig.'

'I hope so,' said Midgley.

Later on he had a cigarette and she had a cake.

'I was certain they were going to ring from the ward,' he said.

'No.' She lifted up the cushion and put the receiver back.

He frowned. Then grinned. 'No harm done,' he said.

They were just settling in again when the phone rang. She answered.

'Yes,' she said, looking at him. 'Yes.'

'What's the matter?' said Midgley.

She put the phone down and looked away.

He was already out of bed and pulling his trousers on.

'Had she rung before?'

She had turned to face the wall.

'Had she?' Midgley was shouting. 'Was she ringing?'

'Don't shout. There are night nurses asleep.'

At the end of the long corridor the doors burst open.

'It's the biggest wonder I'd not gone into see Mrs Tunnicliffe,' said Aunty Kitty. 'She's in Ward 7 with her hip. She's been waiting two years. But I don't know what it was. Something made me come back upstairs. I was sat looking at a *Woman's Own* then in walks Joyce and next minute the nurse is calling us in and he has his eyes open! So we were both there, weren't we.'

Mrs Midgley nodded. They were all three stood by the bedside.

'He just said, "Is our Denis here? Is our Denis here?"' said Aunty Kitty, 'and I said: "He's just coming, Frank." And he smiled a little smile and it was all over. Bless him. I was his only sister.'

The body lay flat on the bed, the eyes closed, the sheet up to the neck.

'The dot does something different when you're dying,' said Aunty Kitty, looking at the screen which now showed a continuous line. 'I wasn't watching it, naturally, but I noticed out of the corner of my eye it was doing something different during the last moments.'

'I think he's smiling,' said Mrs Midgley.

'Of course he's smiling,' said Midgley. He went and looked out of the window. 'He's won. Scored. In the last minute of extra time.'

Mrs Midgley came over to the window and said in an undertone: 'You disgust me.'

A nurse came in and switched off the monitor.

They went out.

'It's a pity you weren't here, Denis,' said Aunty Kitty. 'I mean when it came to the crunch. You've been so good. You've been here all the time he was dying. What were you doing?'

'Living,' said Midgley.

'He's at peace anyway,' said Aunty Kitty.

They went out and got his clothes. As they were walking out a young man was on the phone. 'It's a boy!' he was saying. 'A boy! Yes. Just think. I'm a father.'

They stood in the car park.

'I suppose while we're here,' said Joyce, 'we could go up home and make a start on going through his things.'

AFTERWORD

Father! Father! Burning Bright was the original title of a BBC television film I wrote in 1982 but which was subsequently entitled *Intensive Care*. The main part, Midgley, had been hard to cast, though when I was writing the script I thought it was a role I might play myself until, that is, I got to the scene where Midgley goes to bed with Valery, the slatternly nurse. That, I thought, effectively ruled me out as I didn't fancy having to take my clothes off under the bored appraisal of an entire film crew.

Not that it would have been the first time. Back in 1966 I was acting in a BBC TV comedy series I had written which included a weekly spot, 'Life and Times in NW1', in one episode of which I was supposedly in bed with a neighbour's wife. The scene was due to be shot in the studio immediately after a tea break, and rather than brave the scrutiny of the TV crew, I thought that during the break I might sneak on to the set and be already in bed when the crew returned. So I tiptoed into the studio in my underpants, failing to notice that a lighting rig had been positioned behind the bedroom door. When I opened it there was an almighty crash, the lights came down and everybody rushed into the studio to find me sprawled in my underpants among the wreckage and subject to a far more searching and hostile scrutiny than would otherwise have been the case. No more bedroom scenes for me, I thought.

However, the role of Midgley proved hard to cast and after a lot of to-ing and fro-ing, including what was virtually an audition, I found myself playing the part. Like some other leading roles that I have written, it verged on the anonymous, all the fun and jokes put into the mouths of the supporting characters while Midgley, whom the play is supposed to be about, never managed to be much more than morose.

It was in the hope of finding more to the character than this that I decided, before the shooting started, to write the story up in prose. When I'd finished I showed it to the director in the hope that it might help him to appreciate what the screenplay was about. He received it politely enough and in due course gave me it back, I suspect without having read it, directors tending to form their own ideas about a text, one script from the author hard enough to cope with without wanting two.

So I put it away in a drawer in 1982 where it has remained ever since. I've dusted it off and published it now, I suppose, as part of an effort to slim down my *Nachlass* and generally tidy up.